# NOWHERE TO RUN

# nowhere to RUN

CLAIRE J. GRIFFIN

namelos
South Hampton, New Hampshire

First edition

Library of Congress Control Number: 2012951212

ISBN 978-1-60898-144-1 (hardcover : alk. paper)
ISBN 978-1-60898-145-8 (pbk. : alk. paper)
ISBN 978-1-60898-146-5 (ebk.)

www.namelos.com

*For my students at Montgomery College,*
*the ones who inspired me and the ones who drove me crazy.*
*I tried to write a book that you would want to read.*

Life is lived forward
but understood backward.
—*Søren Kierkegaard*

**Two in the morning. One block east of Georgia Avenue. It was**
dangerous for Calvin to be here so late. But he wanted to see Norris,
and everybody knew this side of Georgia was his.

Calvin walked down the street. Row houses were strung along
both sides. Once in a while he passed one that was boarded up, the
yard full of trash and busted lawn chairs. The rest of the houses were
shut tight behind security doors made of half-inch steel bars bent into
fancy shapes.

People's windows were mostly dark, but one or two glowed
with TV light. Maybe a kid, or somebody with no job to get up for the
next morning.

Scraggly trees lined the sidewalk, leaves hanging limp in the
heat. The air hummed with the sound of air conditioners going full
blast. August in D.C. was hot, even at two a.m.

Calvin walked in the middle of the street so he could be seen.
He did not want Norris to think he was sneaking up on him. That
wouldn't be smart.

Calvin wore a white T-shirt, black basketball shorts, and his
favorite running shoes. Just in case.

He knew he could outrun Norris if he had to. After all, Calvin
was a track star. A sprinter. Norris was an out-of-shape hustler
smoking two packs a day. Norris's boys couldn't catch Calvin either.
Nobody could.

Calvin didn't plan on running tonight. Not unless he had to. He
was here to tell Norris not to come around his momma's nail shop
again. Not to go telling Momma she had to give Norris a hundred
dollars.

Calvin was scared, some, going up against Norris. But along
with that, Calvin felt pretty good. He had that adrenaline high he
always got before he raced. Like he could do anything.

Calvin spotted a metal sign hanging off a telephone pole about
eleven feet off the ground. He veered toward it, jumped, and slapped
it with his fingertips. He was ready.

When he landed, Norris was right there in front of him, two of his boys backing him up. They must've been standing behind that old Dodge van.

Norris was light-skinned, with a shaved head and pale eyes that looked right through you and didn't blink.

"Out for a walk, Calvin?" Norris asked in his soft voice.

"Thought I'd get some exercise."

"Don't see you much over here."

"We each got our place."

"That's right. And this ain't yours. So, what you want?"

"You know."

"What if I do?"

"Listen, Norris."

"That ain't my name," Norris whispered. "It's Norris P."

Calvin nodded. "Norris P. Look, you and me, we never had any problems. Let's not start. You're a businessman. I respect that. But I want you to leave my momma outta your business."

Norris's thugs circled behind Calvin. He felt a flicker of fear. Too late to run. It looked like the best he could hope for now would be to go one-on-one with Norris. Even with the other two out of it, Norris was gonna beat the shit out of him. But if Calvin was lucky, the damage wouldn't be permanent. And if he took it like a man, Norris would respect him. Maybe enough to leave Momma alone.

"C'mon, Norris P. Just you and me. Let's do it."

"Okay. Just you and me."

Norris grinned. He'd been keeping his right hand behind his leg. Now he moved just enough for Calvin to see the dull gleam of a metal baseball bat. Calvin broke a sweat.

Norris held the bat loose and let it swing back and forth. Calvin watched his fingers, waiting for them to tighten on the handle so he'd know which way to jump.

Norris leaned his head to one side and narrowed his eyes at Calvin, sizing him up.

"Kneecaps," one of his boys said.

Norris nodded. "Calvin, you been thinkin' 'bout gettin' yourself a track scholarship to some cracker-ass college somewhere?"

Calvin shook his head, not trusting his voice. He hadn't been thinking about college. But he was counting on winning the 100-meter dash at the District Championship in May. He'd been dreaming about it every day for three whole years. Ever since Coach Wilson told him he had a chance.

For Calvin a bat was way worse than a knife.

Norris was saying, "Or maybe I should mess up your face. Bust those nice teeth you got. Somethin' like that."

Calvin had been in his share of fights. He decided to head-butt Norris. Break his nose. Get in close before he had a chance to swing the bat. Calvin would have to take his chances after that. His body tensed.

"Hey, cuz! What's goin' on?"

Somebody moved into the bright circle of streetlight. It was Deej, Calvin's best friend and Norris's cousin.

Deej went up to Norris, gave him the handshake, the knuckle slide. Then he turned and did the same to Calvin.

"Go home, Deej," Norris said. "We're in the middle of somethin'."

"I can see that." Deej draped his arm over Calvin's shoulders. "But Calvin and me, we got a music gig in two weeks. Tonya's turnin' sixteen. Her auntie's payin' us fifty each to play her party. Everybody's gonna be there. This boy's mouth is all busted up, I'll have to find me a new partner."

"I'll just do his knees then."

"No." Deej shook his head, lifting dozens of tiny twists of hair into the air, a labor of love by his latest girlfriend. "We ain't just singin'. We got some steps too."

"I gotta do somethin'."

"How 'bout lettin' Calvin keep his knees on loan?"

"Meanin' what?"

"Meanin' you let him walk," Deej explained, "and then his knees owe you. Like maybe he's favored to win the District Championship next spring. Some dudes are layin' bets. You say Calvin's gonna lose. And he does."

"So?"

"You win some change. Add to your bad-ass rep. Everybody

knows Calvin's s'posed to win. But he doesn't. On account of you own his knees."

"I own Calvin's knees." Norris said the words slowly, like they tasted good in his mouth. He smiled and nodded. "Okay, Deej. I like that." He glared at Calvin. "Don't forget, punk."

Deej's arm tightened around Calvin's neck. "C'mon, bro."

They walked off, Calvin whispering, "Why'd you say that? 'Bout throwin' the race."

"It's hard gettin' Cousin Norris to back down. He's stubborn. But he loves thinkin' he's The Man. So we make it seem like he's got power over you. Don't mean he does."

"Yeah, but..."

"Cousin Norris thinks he owns your knees, so now he'll look out for you."

"What makes you think I want Norris P lookin' out for me?"

"You don't have any choice, Calvin. You can either have him comin' after you with a baseball bat, or you can have him givin' you some space. Which one you want?"

Calvin shrugged off Deej's arm and turned to face him. "I ain't losin' that race. That's all I'm sayin'."

"Take it easy, man. I know that," Deej said. "You like bein' in front the whole way. I know all 'bout that. Ain't I seen every one of your big races? Like the championship last year. You were flyin'!"

They started walking again.

"Eleven point zero six seconds. My best time ever."

"Too bad that senior from Roosevelt leaned across the finish line 'fore you."

"That senior is graduated. This year it's gonna be me."

Calvin tripped on a crack in the sidewalk. Deej grabbed him and kept him on his feet.

"That hot-shot new mayor oughta send some workers out here and fix up these cracks," Deej said. "Somebody's gonna get hurt one of these days."

"Yeah. That's how come this is a dangerous neighborhood. It's on account of the sidewalks."

They laughed. Then Calvin got serious again.

"We still got ourselves a problem, Deej."

"What's that?"

"Nobody bets on D.C. track no more. There used to be some action. Back in the day. But not now."

"Cousin Norris better not find out. He'd really come after you then."

"Why not come after you?"

"We're family."

Calvin nodded, then said, "Anyway, Deej, I owe you big."

"That's all right." Deej paused. "Why you over here anyways?"

"Norris P came into Momma's shop last week. Got her to give him some money."

"Or she'd get her windows all busted in?"

"Somethin' like that," Calvin said.

"Whyn't you tell me?"

"Wanted to take care of it myself."

Deej frowned and shook his head. "Cousin Norris is a real mean mother. You know that, Calvin."

"Lucky for me you came along."

"Luck had nothin' to do with it. I saw you pass Granny Henry's place and started after you. 'Bout a block behind you."

"How come you didn't give me a shout?"

"You know it ain't good to be loud on the street so late. And I figured if you wanted me along, you woulda asked me. But then I saw Cousin Norris with that bat of his."

"You been watchin' my back the whole time?"

"That's right, bro." Deej grinned. "I'm like your guardian angel."

He put his arm over Calvin's shoulder, and they started walking again.

"And don't worry none 'bout Cousin Norris. Your knees gonna be fine. The track championship ain't till spring. By then, Norris'll prob'ly be back in jail. You gonna win, Calvin. You gonna win this time for sure."

**Two blocks before Georgia Avenue, they reached the house Deej** lived in with Granny Henry and his two half-sisters, Danette and Shania. They were older than Deej. All three of them had the same mom. But she didn't come around much anymore.

"Stop by tomorrow night," Deej said. "About eight. We'll go up to the track, and I'll help you with your workout."

"Yeah. Later, man."

Calvin turned south when he got to Georgia. Suddenly he was tired, the adrenaline rush long gone. All he wanted now was to go home and crawl into bed.

The bars were closed. No one around but a few drunks lying in the doorways. All the stores were shut tight, metal grates locked down over windows and doors. Calvin walked past pawn shops, liquor stores, bars, and strip clubs. Spanish markets, Caribbean take-outs, and West African hair-braiding salons. Storefront churches, fortunetellers, and funeral homes.

One time Deej had said to Calvin that Georgia Avenue was a street where you could find God and the devil sitting right next to each other, like they was old friends. Deej was pleased with himself afterward for saying it. Calvin wasn't sure what it meant, but he never forgot it.

Calvin got to his mother's shop and stopped, just like always. He cupped his hands over his eyes and leaned his forehead against the metal grate that covered the window, making sure everything was okay. Momma didn't have much worth stealing. Two big, padded chairs with those basins for soaking your feet, some cheap little tables on rollers, and a lot of nail products. That was it. The place didn't look like much, but Nail Magick did all right.

Calvin stepped back from the window and saw his reflection. He stopped to check out his smile. He had real nice teeth, just like Norris P said. Calvin liked the shape of his head too, so he kept his hair short.

But the best thing Calvin had going for him was his muscles. He worked out almost every day. He had to. Most people didn't realize how much upper-body strength a sprinter needed. So Calvin was cut, on account of all that training and lifting. He might not have girls hanging all over him the way Deej did. But the ladies liked Calvin just fine.

He gave himself another smile, then walked on down the street and turned right at Albert's Auto Shop. This was where he'd been working for almost three years now, detailing cars after school and in the summer.

Calvin had to be back at Albert's in just six hours. He thought about how tired he was and how nice it'd be if he could somehow get inside the shop and sack out in the back room until nine. But Albert had protection. A ten-foot metal fence, jimmy-proof locks, and a new guard dog named Zipper, some bad-ass mix of Rottweiler and pit bull, plus who knew what else. Calvin headed home.

The porch light was off, so he tried to open the big locks on the front door without waking Momma. But he didn't need to bother. Calvin smelled her cigarette as soon as he stepped into the darkened living room. Then he saw a red glow hanging in the air over Momma's place on the couch. The glow moved, and a lamp switched on.

Momma was a big woman, but she had pretty feet that she was real proud of. Right now they were propped up on a cushion that sat on the coffee table, her freshly painted toenails glistening dark red. A pile of celebrity magazines was in her lap, an open Bible on the table beside her.

"How come you're up?" Calvin asked.

"I couldn't sleep. Where were you?"

"There was somethin' I had to do."

"Come into the light, Calvin. So's I can see you."

He walked over to her, sat on the floor, and tilted his head up. "I'm fine, Momma. See?"

"What were you doing out so late?"

"Don't worry, Momma. It was nothin' illegal."

"Why are you so late?" she repeated.

"I told you. There was somethin' I had to take care of."

*Whack!* Momma hit him on the side of the head with a rolled-up magazine. She did this sometimes, ever since Calvin's father died.

"You listen to me, Calvin. Talking tough's another way to get yourself hurt. So whatever it is you were doing, you drop it. Do you hear me?"

He nodded.

"Say the promise you made to Daddy Lewis before he passed."

"I will graduate high school."

"That's right, baby."

Momma leaned forward and took Calvin's face in her hands. She stroked his cheeks. It felt nice.

"You got to keep yourself safe and out of trouble. You got to avoid even the appearance of trouble."

"It's hard, Momma."

"You think I don't know? That's why you got to be thinking about it all the time. You got to keep your head down. God is looking out for you, baby. But He can't do it alone. You got to give Him all the helps you can."

**Calvin overslept and got to work late. When he walked through the** front door, Albert was standing at the counter looking at the book where he wrote down the day's appointments. He slowly turned his head and stared at the clock on the wall, then looked back at Calvin. Albert didn't say a word. It was ten after nine.

Albert was an interesting guy. A Jamaican hard-ass. Usually those islanders were real laid back, but not Albert. He didn't even sound Jamaican because his family moved to England before he ended up in D.C. He had this classy accent that really threw the customers, especially the white ones.

Besides being Calvin's boss, Albert helped Coach Wilson with the track team at Harry Truman High School. It wasn't a job or anything. Albert volunteered. He'd been a pretty big-time sprinter back in Jamaica.

That's how Calvin and Albert met. From Albert coaching him. Helping him increase his stride length. Improving his form. Making him faster. Albert knew a lot about track.

Later on, when Albert needed help at his shop, Calvin could never figure out why he decided to hire Calvin, out of all the guys on the team that wanted the job. It was a sweet gig, washing and detailing these smooth rides. Thinking maybe someday he'd have one of his own.

Calvin grabbed a pair of clean coveralls from the back room, plus a Styrofoam cup of coffee with milk and four sugars. Then he went on into the garage and said hola to César, who was leaning over the engine of a shiny black Carrera and singing some whiny Latin love song to himself while he worked.

César didn't answer, so Calvin went outside into the car yard and got busy. He was getting a late start, and there was a full schedule of cars for him to finish by quitting time.

He always followed the same order when he worked on a car. First he wiped down everything inside. Then he vacuumed the floors. Next he shampooed the carpets and put leather conditioner on the seats. Almost all the cars that came to Albert's for detailing had full leather interiors. On the outside, he washed and waxed the car, scrubbed the wheels, and wiped some stuff on the tires to make them shiny. The last thing was washing the windows inside and out. The whole job took him about three hours.

By noon, he'd done one car and was starting the second. It was the newest-model Mercedes sedan, navy with a white interior. Sweet.

Albert didn't allow radios or iPods in the shop, so Calvin let his mind drift while he worked.

He remembered last night and how his heart froze up when Norris P said he wanted to break Calvin's knees. He thought about Deej coming along just in time. He thought about how Norris P owned his knees now, and Calvin wasn't sure what that meant. All he knew was that nothing would stop him from winning the 100-meter dash at the championship. Nothing.

Then Calvin remembered his talk with Momma. And that started him thinking about Daddy Lewis and how he looked after the heart attack three years ago. In his mind, he could still see his daddy lying there in the hospital hooked up to all those machines, Momma sitting next to his bed with Little Lewis on her lap.

The doctors all acted like Daddy Lewis was going to pull through and come home again. Nobody had got around to talking about how a man with a bad heart could keep on climbing ladders and painting houses for a living.

But it turned out Daddy Lewis was smarter than the doctors. He must've known what was coming because he made Calvin say those words, about graduating from high school. That night when his daddy's heart stopped, the doctors couldn't get it going again.

Calvin figured he'd make it through until graduation like he promised. That'd make Momma happy. He had to stay in school anyway and get decent grades so he'd be eligible to run in the D.C. Track Championship in May. Nobody knew how bad he wanted to win that 100-meter race. Except Deej, of course.

Up to the race, Calvin's future was clear. The hard part was figuring out what to do after. After the race. After graduation. Albert was always telling him he had to have a plan. But he didn't.

That's what Calvin was thinking while he vacuumed the

Mercedes. Not paying much attention to what he was doing until he spotted something shiny under the accelerator pedal. He picked it up. A woman's earring. It had stones in it that looked like diamonds. There was a big one at the top and some little ones hanging down in a line, each one smaller than the one above it. Calvin wondered if the diamonds were real. Because of the car, he guessed they probably were.

It was almost twelve thirty. Not quite lunchtime. Calvin figured Albert wouldn't mind him quitting five minutes early, not if Calvin showed him the earring.

Calvin went into the office and stood right inside the door under the AC. He unzipped his coveralls and let the air blow on his sweaty T-shirt until he got a nice chill. While he was standing there, Albert walked out of the restroom drying his hands on a paper towel.

"I found this in that Benz out there." Calvin dropped the earring into Albert's hand.

Albert looked at it and then smiled at him. "This does you credit, Calvin. It shows you're an honorable man. And it adds to the sterling reputation of Albert's Auto Shop. That's why all these nice rich people trust us with their fancy cars."

Calvin shook his head and laughed. "Know what, Albert? I never get tired of hearin' you talk."

It was César's turn to go for food, and he came back with sandwiches from the Salvadoran place up the street. Calvin wasn't a big fan of pupusas, but he was always happy to eat one of Mama Pearl's tuna melts.

They all ate together in the back room, Calvin, Albert, and César. They sat on folding chairs pulled up to the rickety table, surrounded by cluttered metal shelves and old car seats with the stuffing coming out.

"Hey, Calvin," César said, talking around a mouthful of food, "Mama Pearl is wonder when you stop order her gringo menu? She wants I tell you her cooking is gooood."

"I know it's good. But there's something about Salvador food. It doesn't agree with me. I like how it tastes, but then it just sits in my stomach all day. I go for my run after a pupusa lunch, and I can hardly move. You know why that is, Albert?"

"I have no idea. But when you're an athlete, one of the things you learn is to listen to your body. If your body says 'No pupusas,' you have to respect that. Doesn't matter why."

"There any food that slows you down, Albert?" Calvin asked.

"I can't eat Chinese. Makes me want to lie down and take a nap."

"You guys are loco," César said, stuffing the last pupusa into his mouth and chewing it down.

After they finished eating, Albert disappeared into his office. Calvin and César sat and talked until he came and told them it was time to get back to work.

"By the way, Calvin," Albert said, "I called that customer and told her that you found her earring. She was very gratified."

"What's gratified mean?" César asked.

"Grateful."

"Then how come you don't say grateful?"

"Because I like saying gratified."

"Why this customer is so grateful?"

"Calvin found her earring."

"Lemme see."

Albert reached into his shirt pocket and pulled it out.

"Is it real?" César asked.

"The customer said it was worth a lot of money. She said to tell you thank you, Calvin."

"But she don't offer no reward," César said.

"No reward. She said she thought she might have lost it in the car and she was hoping we'd find it."

"How come she didn't say anything about it when she brought the car in?" Calvin asked. He felt angry, without knowing why. "What was it? Some kinda test or somethin'?"

Albert smiled one of his high-class smiles. "Everything is a test."

After Albert went back into his office, César turned to Calvin and said, "What are you? Estupido? You shoulda keep it. Pawn it. Or give it your girl."

Calvin didn't answer, just headed back out to finish the Mercedes.

As he rubbed a soapy sponge over the roof of the car, he thought about what Albert said. That everything was a test. Calvin would have to remember to tell that to Deej. Find out what he thought about it.

Calvin finished the car, went looking for Albert, and spotted his skinny legs sticking out from underneath a Navigator. Calvin squatted down beside him.

"Hey, Albert. Thought maybe me and Zipper could get to know each other. Okay if I take him for a walk?"

Albert said it was fine and told him where to find the leash.

Zipper lived in a cage in the front office during the day and roamed around the car yard at night. He was a mean-looking dog. All black with sharp white teeth that could probably take your arm right off. But Calvin wasn't worried. He got along with dogs. He talked in a quiet voice and made sure he moved real slow so Zipper didn't get spooked.

Out on the street, Calvin let Zipper take his time doing whatever he had to do. Afterward, when the dog was back in his cage, he stuck his tongue between the wires and licked Calvin's hands.

"Hey, fella. You smell that tuna melt? Hang on a sec."

Calvin went to the back room, dug through the trash, and returned with what was left of his sandwich. The end of the roll had been soggy, and Calvin hadn't wanted to finish it.

He unwrapped the sandwich and fed it to Zipper, then let him lick the wrapper.

"We'll go out again tomorrow. Okay, buddy?"

Calvin reached into the cage again and gave Zipper a final scratch. Then he headed outside to the yard and worked straight through until he was done with the last car. As he was getting out of his damp coveralls, Albert stuck his head into the back room and asked if he could see Calvin a minute.

Calvin followed Albert into his office and watched him take a key off his desk and hold it out.

"What's that?"

"The key to the shop."

"What're you givin' me a key for?"

"There's construction all around my new condo. If I get stuck in traffic some morning, I want you to open up for me."

"The customers only wanna talk to you, Albert."

"Well, if I'm not here, they're going to have to talk to you. Just explain it to them, Calvin. Be polite. You're good at that. Have them tell you what the problem is and let them see you write it down. Get their phone number. And tell them I'll call them as soon as I get in."

Calvin reached for the key. "Okay, I guess I can do that."

**Most Tuesdays and Thursdays, Calvin and Deej met at the school**
track for a nighttime workout. They'd started doing it last year, before
the District Championship. It had been Albert's idea. The main thing
was for Deej to help Calvin stay motivated. Albert explained how
much easier it was to work out when you had a regular schedule and
someone to coach you through it when it got hard.

And it worked. Last year, when Calvin was just a junior, he'd
almost won the 100-meter dash. He was beat out at the finish by the
senior from Roosevelt, but no one expected it to even be close.

This year Calvin would win that race. Unless Norris P ordered
him to lose. Calvin didn't know what he'd do if that happened. But he
didn't need to think about that right now. The championship was still
a long way off. What he needed to be thinking about now was how to
make himself the fastest sprinter in Washington D.C.

Last night, when they were walking home after seeing Norris P,
Deej had said to Calvin, "You gonna win this time for sure."

Those words had sounded good. Calvin was saying them to
himself now, pushing to run up the concrete bleachers one last time. He
was trying to break through the wall of what he thought he could do, his
lungs burning, his heart beating like it would jump right out of his chest,
his legs so tired he could hardly lift them. And every few steps, whenever
he was ready to ease up, ready to give in to how tired he was, he'd say
those words, loud and clear, inside his head. *You gonna win this time.
You gonna win.*

Then, inside his dark world of pain and exhaustion, Calvin
heard a different voice that sounded like it came from the end of a
long tunnel. It was Deej calling up to him.

"That's right, Calvin. Lift your knees. Use your arms. I know
you're tired. But keep it long. Push off with your back foot. When you
get to the top, wait for me."

Calvin reached the last step and grabbed hold of the metal
railing that went along the top of the stands. He took huge, ragged
breaths. It seemed like there wasn't enough air in the whole world to
fill up his lungs. Deej jogged up the steps.

"How you feelin', Calvin? You doin' okay?"

Calvin let go of the railing. He leaned over, head down, hands on his knees to hold himself up. Sweat rolled off his face and dripped onto the concrete, making a dark puddle between his feet.

Deej rested his hand lightly on Calvin's back. "You doin' good, Calvin. Real good. Let me know when you're ready for some water. It's hot."

Silently, Calvin straightened and reached for the water bottle. His breathing was starting to even out, but he still didn't have enough air to talk. He rinsed his mouth, then spat over the back of the stands.

"C'mon, Calvin. Walk around some. Get rid of that lactic acid Albert told us about, or you'll be sore tomorrow."

Calvin walked back and forth behind the last row of seats. After a while he could talk.

He held up the bottle. "We got plenty, right?"

"Yeah."

Calvin squeezed water over his face and head, then shook himself and grinned. "I hate it when you make me run bleachers."

Deej grinned back. "I know."

Calvin took a deep breath and let it out, slow and steady. He nodded. "Okay. I'm ready. Let's go down."

Usually after Calvin's workout he and Deej hung out on the football field and talked while Calvin stretched. This was a time he always liked. Calvin was tired, but he felt great. He used to think it was just being glad he was done with his workout. Then Deej told him it was all about some chemicals that got in his blood after he exercised, called endolphins or something like that.

But this time Deej said he couldn't stay.

"Where you off to?" Calvin asked.

"No place special."

Calvin had been sitting on the grass with his legs straight in front of him, leaning forward and holding on to his ankles, making his favorite stretch last another few seconds. Now he straightened up and said, "Guess I'll just head home then. I'm beat. Didn't get much sleep last night."

"Yeah." Deej turned to go. Then he paused and turned back.

"Listen. There's somethin' I wanna say 'bout that."

Calvin waited.

"Stay clear of Cousin Norris. He's mean all the way through."

"But you hang with him sometimes."

"There's lotsa reasons for that."

"Like what?"

"First, he's my cousin. So he'd never really do me dirty 'cause he knows Granny Henry would call him out with my uncles. He wouldn't like that. They're tougher'n him."

Calvin started packing up his gym bag. "So tell me another reason."

"Whadya mean?"

"You said there's lots of reasons it's okay for you to hang with Norris P. Tell me another one."

"Sometimes we do a little business together."

Calvin stopped what he was doing and looked up from his bag. "That doesn't sound too good, Deej. What kinda business?"

"Sometimes he pays me to do a little job. Somethin' he wants to keep in the family."

Calvin stuck his face close to his friend's. "Be careful. Norris P's done some serious jail time. You know that. He's a criminal."

"Not just a criminal. Cousin Norris is vicious." Deej shrugged. "That's his rep, anyways. Personally, I never seen him do nothin' so bad. When me and him are together, I think he tries to keep things pretty clean. But you hear stuff. You know?"

"Then you shouldn't be hangin' out with him."

"I told you. There's reasons."

Calvin yanked the zipper shut. "You mean reasons like the new AC you bought Granny Henry? I wondered about that."

"She needed one. I gotta take care of that old lady. She's been good to me."

"I don't like it, Deej."

"Don't worry about it."

"You said so yourself—Norris P is vicious. Doesn't matter if he's your cousin or not."

"It's okay, Calvin. I can handle Cousin Norris."

"What makes you so sure?"

" 'Cause I'm smarter'n him. Look what happened last night. You still got both your knees, right?"

Calvin couldn't think of anything to say to that.

5

**Tonya's aunts had the back yard set up nice for her birthday.** There were little white lights strung along the fence and Japanese lanterns hanging from the roof of the back porch.

That's where Calvin and Deej set up Deej's new speakers and an iPod downloaded with their own mix. They had about nine hours of music, mellow at the start so people could eat and talk, then solid dance music later on. In between, for when they sang, they'd laid down some tracks without any vocals.

Calvin could tell right away it was going to be a special night. School was starting in four days, so this was the last big bang of summer. And since it was hot out, all the ladies were showing plenty of skin.

Low-cut tank tops. Strapless tube tops. Tiny skirts and shorts. Bare backs and shoulders. Long legs that ended in painted toenails and sexy sandals. Calvin was into women's summer fashion in a big way.

There was just one problem. A week ago Deej had told Calvin's little brother that he could perform with them. Calvin wasn't happy when he found out.

"Why'd you tell Little Lewis it was okay?" he'd asked Deej.

"It's important to him."

"So?"

"C'mon, Calvin. He just wants to be like you. That's all."

"He's only eight. He'll mess up."

"No, he won't. He can sing just fine. You know that. And he's been showin' me his dance moves. He's pretty good."

"I don't like it."

"It'll be fine. The girls'll dig it. You'll see."

Which meant that at the party Little Lewis wouldn't leave them alone. He was so excited, Calvin thought he might float away over their heads, like a balloon or something.

About every ten minutes Little Lewis bounced up to Deej and said, "Is it time? I mean I know it isn't. But be sure you tell me. I want to be ready. I mean I'm ready now. If you asked me to go on right now, I'd be ready. Just tell me when it's time. Okay, Deej?"

Deej put his hand on Little Lewis's shoulder, weighing him down. "Hey, little dude. Can you still feel the ground?"

Little Lewis bent his knees, shuffled his feet. "Yeah, I can feel it."

"That's good. Every once in a while, check your feet. Make sure you can feel the ground."

"Okay, Deej."

"Now go off and get somethin' to eat. And drink some water. Your mouth's gonna get real dry right before you sing."

Little Lewis danced off, and Calvin called after him, "That's right. Keep yourself hydrated. Same as what I do at a track meet."

Little Lewis turned and looked at Calvin with big old eyes, like an owl. "Okay, Calvin," he said, then ran off.

Calvin never had much appetite before he sang, but he thought he could maybe eat a piece of fried chicken. He wandered over to the tables where the food was laid out.

That's when he saw Norris P standing alone over by the fence. He had his hands in his pockets. Designer shades covered his eyes, so Calvin couldn't tell who he was looking at, whether it was Calvin or somebody else.

While Calvin watched, Deej went over to his cousin, and they left the back yard together, walking fast like they were in a hurry to get away from the party. Calvin thought maybe they were arguing about something. Then they moved across the street behind some parked cars, and he couldn't see them anymore.

Calvin grabbed a beer from one of the coolers and went inside to find the bathroom. When he came out, Deej was back in the crowd again. Calvin could see him talking to a bunch of girls and making them laugh. Norris was gone.

One of the girls standing with Deej had her back to Calvin. Even from behind she looked good. She was wearing a stretchy, off-the-shoulder orange top, and her hair was twisted on top of her head and held there with some kind of fancy hair clip. When Calvin walked up and she turned to look at him, her beaded earrings brushed against her bare shoulders.

Deej was saying something, but Calvin didn't hear.

"Don't mind my friend," Deej said. "He's not as stupid as he looks."

Calvin still couldn't talk.

"I'd say you definitely made an impression on him, though. The dude is speechless. You usually have that effect on a man, Junior?"

That last piece of information got through to Calvin. "Junior? Your name is Junior?" he asked.

She laughed. She had a pretty mouth. "That's my high school nickname. I eat a box of Junior Mints every day for lunch."

"What high school?"

"Out in Chicago. I was just there for a year. Before that I was here. I guess you don't remember me."

"I'm pretty sure I'd remember you."

Deej was trying not to laugh.

"What's so funny?" Calvin asked.

"This is Wade Martin's baby sister!" Deej announced.

"You mean the dude that's drivin' around somewhere on a Navy submarine? That the Wade Martin you mean?"

"Yeah."

"No way. Wade's sister was a year younger'n us. And she was a skinny little thing. No shape on her at all."

This time Deej did laugh.

"Wait. You mean you're what's-her-name?" Calvin thought hard for a couple of seconds. "Carla?"

Junior nodded.

"Carla had what they call a growth spurt," Deej said as he slipped his arm around Junior's waist.

Junior ignored Deej and kept her eyes on Calvin. "I have an aunt in Chicago. She had a baby, but she needed to keep her job. Working nights. She's a nurse. I went out to help her with the baby."

"That's nice. You goin' to Harry Truman?"

"No, my daddy is sending me to Saint Bernadette's."

Calvin nodded. "That's a good idea. Things can get pretty crazy over at HT."

After that, he tried hard to think of something else to say, just so he could keep looking into her eyes. They were brown with little specks of gold in them.

Junior's mouth lifted at the corners. Her eyes smiled up at him.

She held out her hand. It was small and soft and warm. "It was nice talking to you, Calvin."

Calvin watched Junior disappear into the crowd. "What a disaster," he said to Deej.

Deej put his arm around Calvin's neck. "No man, she dug you. I could tell. And wait till she sees your stuff." He guided Calvin toward the back porch. "C'mon. It's time."

"Hang on. I gotta find Little Lewis."

Naturally, Little Lewis was nowhere around now that they needed him. When he finally turned up, Calvin and Deej were already up on the porch, checking their set-up one last time. Then they started singing.

Deej was right. When Little Lewis joined in, the ladies loved it. They made that little "aw" sound they always do when they see a cute puppy or a baby or something.

Calvin could see Junior standing with some other girls. There was one time he looked right at her and nodded. She smiled back and gave a little wave.

The last song they did was a new and improved version of "Happy Birthday." They finished it off with some dancing that featured Little Lewis doing all his best moves.

At the end, when everybody was still clapping, Tonya's aunts brought out a cake with sparklers on it. This time the whole crowd sang.

While her grandmother was cutting the cake and getting it passed, Tonya wobbled up onto the porch and threw her arms around them, one at a time. She'd had too much to drink. While she was giving Calvin a sloppy kiss, he looked over her shoulder and saw Junior frowning and shaking her head.

As soon as Tonya turned her attention to Deej, Calvin went up to Junior. She handed him a plate of food.

"What's this?"

"Deej said you never can eat before you sing. They were starting to run out of chicken, so I asked Tonya's aunt to save some for you."

Calvin peeled back the foil. The plate was piled with fried chicken, potato salad, collards, baked beans, and cole slaw.

"This is a lot of food. Gonna take me a while. You sure you don't mind if I eat?"

Junior tilted her head and smiled. "That's why I saved it for you."

Calvin started spooning potato salad into his mouth, trying not to look like a pig. He didn't want to end up with food all over his face.

"You and Deej were really good up there," Junior said. "And that was your little brother?"

Calvin nodded, his mouth full.

"He's a good dancer."

Calvin was about to take another bite of chicken, but instead he dropped the piece back onto his plate. "Why didn't you say you wanted to dance?"

"That's not what I said. Take your time. It's all right, Calvin."

"It's not all right for me to keep you waitin' like this. I can eat later."

"I don't mind. Honest."

"Don't you wanna dance?"

Junior laughed. "Okay then. Yes, I do want to dance. I've just been waiting for the right person to ask me."

6

**Calvin woke up in a good mood the next morning, so he asked his** brother if he wanted to shoot some hoops. Little Lewis ran upstairs to get his ball before Calvin changed his mind.

As they headed out the door, Calvin grabbed the ball from Lewis and started dribbling down the sidewalk. "C'mon, little brother. Try and steal it off me."

Calvin dribbled low, so Lewis thought he had a chance. He made a grab for the ball, but Calvin switched hands. Then he went between his legs. Spun right. Spun left.

"Stop showin' off!" Little Lewis shouted.

"I'm just feelin' good. That's all."

"I know why."

"Why?"

" 'Cause of Junior." Little Lewis said it like *Jooooonior* and followed it up with a lot of kissing noises.

Calvin laughed.

"You gonna see her again?"

"I might see her today. She said she'd call."

But she didn't.

Four o'clock came, and Calvin had gone for a run, lifted weights in the basement, taken a shower, driven Momma to the grocery, and played a couple hours of "Madden." He was back in the basement with his shirt off, doing extra sets of pull-ups, when his cell went off. He got to it on the second ring.

"Calvin?"

"Deej? Oh man! I thought you was Junior."

"Listen, Calvin. There's somethin' I didn't tell you last night. 'Bout Junior. She's got one of them Doberman daddies. Sends her to Catholic school. Keeps track of where she goes, who she hangs with. I was surprised she was even at that party last night. 'Cause Tonya's not exactly a nun."

"What're you sayin'?"

"I'm just tellin' you. So you know."

"I really wanna see her, Deej. What should I do?"

"I don't know much 'bout girls that come with a daddy attached," Deej said. "But my guess is you gotta treat Junior like a princess. 'Cause that's how her daddy sees her."

"How do I do that?"

"The princess don't make the call. The princess sits at home with her daddy and hopes the phone rings."

"And it's the prince calling?"

"That's right."

Calvin started to laugh but ended up groaning like he was in pain. "I can't call her! I never got her number."

"That's okay. 'Cause I did."

"When'd you do that?"

"You were inside the house. It was before you even saw her."

"You were gonna call her?"

"I was thinkin' I might. 'Cause she's so gorgeous and all. But she's not really my type. And later on everybody could see how much you two dug each other."

The number Junior gave Deej was her house phone. Even though she had a cell, it turned out she wasn't allowed to give a boy her number until her daddy met him.

When Calvin finally got up the nerve to call Junior's house, it was her daddy who answered. But that was okay. Calvin was ready because Deej had made him practice what he'd say to Junior's daddy. Just in case.

"Hello," said a deep voice. It sounded enough like when Deej was pretending to be Junior's daddy that it was almost funny, and Calvin forgot to be nervous. Slowly and clearly, he said the exact words he and Deej had spent half an hour deciding were the right ones.

"Hello, sir. This is Calvin Williams. Is, um, Carla available, please?"

"I'll see." There was a pause, and then the voice added, "By the way, young man, my wife and I are aware of the fact that our daughter is nicknamed after a box of movie candy. Even her mother calls her Junior now. But I will continue to call her Carla."

Junior must have been standing right there because the next voice Calvin heard was hers.

"Hi, Calvin."

For a second Calvin was speechless, just like at the party. Then he decided to go ahead and tell her what was going through his mind.

"I like how you say my name."

"Is there something different about it?"

"No. But it sounds special 'cause you're the one saying it."

Junior laughed. "Have you been taking lessons in talking smooth from your friend Deej?"

"No. I thought of that just now. All by myself."

"Uh-huh."

"I can tell you don't believe me. Here's somethin' else you won't believe."

"What's that?"

"This afternoon me and Deej spent half an hour rehearsing what I was gonna say if your daddy answered the phone."

Junior laughed again. "I know he can be scary. But whatever you said, it must've been okay. That joke he made about my nickname? That's Daddy being friendly. He only says it if he likes you. If he thinks you're not polite enough, he just hangs up. But first he tells you not to call back."

"And you're okay with that?"

"I know girls who've gotten involved with some bad guys. I know one girl with a boyfriend who got so jealous he tried to run her over. But I don't have to worry about any of that. Those guys don't get past my daddy."

"What's your mom like?"

"She's really sweet. But Daddy's definitely the boss."

"So I'm guessin' if you and me are gonna be spendin' time together, I need to come over and meet your parents."

"That's right."

"Can I come now?"

"No, it's after nine. Too late."

"How 'bout tomorrow."

"No way! Your school doesn't start till next week, but at Saint

Bernadette's we start the day after tomorrow. I'm not allowed to do any socializing on a school night."

"Girl, you are not makin' this easy."

7

**School started. Calvin's senior year.**

On the first day, he got his schedule, tried out his classes. There was one young history teacher who seemed okay, but he didn't even have enough books for the whole class. Which was business as usual at Harry Truman High School.

On the second day, Mr. Nurch, this year's new principal, made an announcement on the loudspeaker that they were taking all the sodas out of the machines and putting in healthy drinks instead, on account of they were worried about students getting fat and having too many cavities. Calvin thought this was really stupid.

He tried to explain it to Junior as he walked with her from Saint Bernadette's to the library where she liked to study until dinner. This short walk was the only time she was allowed to see Calvin during the week.

"Why don't you think taking out the sodas is a good idea?" Junior asked.

"C'mon, you know how it is at HT. Kids are always beatin' up on each other. In the lavatories. On the stairs. The whole place is full of weapons. Isn't that way worse for my health than drinkin' soda? But Nurch isn't doin' anything to make the school any safer."

"What could he do?"

"Prob'ly nothin'. We already got security guards and scanners. Trouble is most of the time the guards are just blabbin' at each other, specially the women. They're not even lookin' at the scanners when the kids put their stuff through. I've seen a knife or some brass knuckles go by, right up there on the screen. The guards never do anything. It's a joke."

"Nurch could do something about that. He could get the guards to pay better attention."

"Except it won't make any difference. There's no way they can keep guns and knives outta school. Not if kids wanna bring 'em. But it still makes me mad. 'Cause that's what they should be worryin' about, not what kinda drinks they put in the soda machines."

This walk with Junior was the best part of Calvin's day. He

loved being with her, having his arm around her waist, their bodies bumping softly with every step.

"So tell me about your day," Calvin said.

"Jenna and Semeka are in my U.S. history class. I think I told you already that they're my two best friends. And we've got a project together. We're excited because we've already got some good ideas."

"You really like school, don't you?"

"Uh-huh. My teachers say I have a curious mind."

"I thought it was just your parents makin' you work so hard."

"What I like best is history. Do you like history, Calvin?"

"It's all right."

"I like finding out how things were a long time ago. Or how things were in other places. I want to go to college and teach history someday."

"You got a plan for yourself."

"Uh-huh."

"I never spent time with a girl that had plans. Your whole way of lookin' at things is different."

"Don't you have plans, Calvin?"

"Not really."

"But you're going to graduate. And you're working hard to get faster so you can win the 100-meter dash in the District Championship."

"Well, yeah. I'm gonna do both those things. But after that, I just don't know."

"You could go to community college and get a degree in automotive repair. Then you could be Albert's mechanic. Maybe someday have your own car shop."

"I'm not much for school, Junior. Graduatin' high school is one thing. Pretty much all you have to do is show up to class and stay outta trouble. But college? I don't think so."

"At least you have a real job."

"And I have you, girl."

They both stopped walking and turned toward each other. They kissed, long and slow. Calvin brushed Junior's hair off her face and looked into her eyes.

"You're all I need," he told her.

Calvin's daily walk with Junior never gave them more than twenty minutes together, no matter how slowly they tried to go. But Junior said her daddy thought the arrangement was "appropriate." Later on she reported he'd smiled when she told him Calvin had started carrying her backpack.

Calvin did other things too that showed how much he respected Junior, that he thought she was a princess. He was always on time when he picked her up to go see a movie or a football game. And if they were driving somewhere, he'd open the car door for her because he figured her daddy would be watching from the window.

Deej started teasing him. "Brother, you are really down with this whole respect thing. That daddy of hers must love you."

"The thing is, I do respect her. I still can't believe Junior is even my girlfriend. So bein' nice to her is easy. The hard part is sittin' in her living room and makin' conversation with her parents while she's upstairs gettin' ready to go out."

Deej winced. "They ask you lotsa questions?"

Calvin nodded. "It's like I'm slowly givin' that man my whole life story. He knows all about Daddy Lewis and the heart attack. And about Momma and Nail Magick. And Little Lewis. Workin' for Albert. Running. Everything."

Deej shook his head. "Don't think I could ever like a girl enough to go through that."

"The first couple times, it was awful. Thought I'd sweat right through my shirt."

"Sounds painful, but it'll pay off 'cause soon her daddy's gonna start givin' you more freedom. Then you won't have to keep spendin' money on actual dates. It's kinda like you're a businessman. You're makin' an investment. That's real smart, Calvin."

"That's not why I'm doin' it."

"Don't make no difference," Deej said.

8

**Deej was right. Little by little, Junior's daddy let them spend more** time together. Then, one Saturday night, after a phone conversation early in the week to make sure Momma would be there, he let Junior come over to Calvin's house. From seven until ten, sharp.

Momma cleaned the whole house and told Calvin she and Little Lewis would watch TV and play board games upstairs.

"I promised Junior's daddy you'd stay out of your bedroom," she warned, "but you can have the living room to yourselves."

All of a sudden Calvin started to worry that being alone with Junior for three whole hours might be awkward at first. So at the last minute he called Deej and asked him to come over for a while.

"You crazy?" Deej laughed. "After all you went through so you two could be alone together?"

"Listen, it's not like me and Junior are goin' to have sex or anything."

"I know, Calvin. You got that whole respect thing goin' on. And I admire that. I really do. But there must be somethin' you been thinkin' 'bout doin'. What about that Tamara girl, the end of last year? You two couldn't keep your hands off each other."

"Junior's not like Tamara. Anyway, I just want you here early on."

Deej laughed. "I never figured myself as no chaperone. But I'll do it 'cause it's you askin'."

"You ever need me to chaperone you, Deej, I'm there for you."

"I'll keep that in mind." Deej paused. "Now what are you-all gonna do? Rent a movie?"

"I guess."

"Hang on a sec. Didn't you say Junior just got a fancy new laptop?"

"Yeah. To help with her homework."

"Have her bring it. And she can tell that daddy of hers that she is gonna have a very educational evening."

Junior drove over to Calvin's house after dinner. Calvin had offered to pick her up, but she explained that her daddy wanted her to have his car. "Just in case."

"Just in case what?" Calvin asked.

"In case Junior needs to make a quick getaway," Deej said, and they all laughed. They were standing in the tiny front hall of Calvin's house. Junior was wearing black cropped pants and a hot-pink top. Her computer bag hung from her shoulder.

Deej looked at her and said, "You sure look good in that outfit, Junior. Although I am kinda disappointed you're not wearin' your school uniform. You know what Calvin told me the first time he saw you in that? He said—"

"He said, 'Who knew a plaid skirt and a pair of knee socks could get a dude's mind goin' like that,' " Junior finished up. "See? Calvin tells me everything."

Deej shook his head in amazement. "This girl is somethin' else, Calvin. You better hang on to her. Not let some other guy steal her off you."

"That won't happen," Junior said softly, stepping close to Calvin so he could put his arms around her.

"Okay, you two. That's enough. Don't wanna have to report you to Junior's daddy or nothin'. Write you up. I promised this evening would be educational."

"Uh-huh," Junior said. She was smiling as she pulled her laptop out of its case. "When I told Daddy, he said he wanted to hear all about it."

"Come over here to the couch," Deej said. "No, I better sit in the middle."

When they were arranged on the couch with the laptop open on Deej's lap, he said, "Now isn't this nice?" and burst out laughing.

"Quit bein' a clown and tell me what we're doin'," Calvin said, but he was laughing too.

Deej turned to Junior. "Calvin's a big-time sprinter. You know all about that, right?"

"Yes, I do."

"But do you know anything about sprinting?"

Junior shook her head. "Not really."

"See? That's what I mean. If you're gonna be Calvin's girlfriend, you need to learn a few things." Deej turned on the laptop.

"How will you find a network?" Junior asked. "You don't have a computer, do you, Calvin?"

He shook his head. "Deej is a computer hot-shot. He'll get us on."

Deej tapped the keyboard for half a minute and then said, "There. You see? Nothin' to it." He tapped some more. "I was on the school computers the other day and found all these dope track videos. I mean I watch YouTube a lot at school. But I never thought to look for anything about track. Which was kinda dumb. Turns out YouTube has all kinds of track stuff."

"Like what?" Junior asked.

"Training videos. Drills. Exercises. Races from the World Championships and the Olympics. Famous runners. Everything."

"That's cool," Calvin said.

"Yeah. Some of this stuff could really help us," Deej said. "Course you'll wanna check it out with Coach Wilson or Albert first. Make sure we don't add any drills they don't want you doin'." Deej elbowed Junior. "See? I told you it was gonna be educational. So, Calvin, what you wanna show her first?"

"How 'bout some of the great runners?"

"Like Usain Bolt?" Deej asked. "World's fastest man? Only guy to ever break his own Olympic record?"

Calvin turned to Junior and explained, "Bolt is incredible. He ran the 100 meters in 9.69 seconds in 2008. And then he ran it in 9.63 in 2012. He's the greatest sprinter ever."

Deej jumped in. "The 2012 race was the fastest in history. Almost every runner did it in less than ten seconds. And Bolt still finished way out in front. He's cocky, though."

"How is he cocky?" Junior asked.

"Keeps tellin' everybody he's a legend," Calvin said. "That sort of thing."

"Okay, so we'll show her Bolt for sure. Who else?" Deej asked. "Greene. Right?"

When Calvin nodded, Deej whispered to Junior, "Calvin's got a soft spot for Maurice Greene."

"He was the world's fastest man until Bolt came along," Calvin explained. "Maurice set a record that lasted nine years."

"Set the record for bein' cocky too. He was way worse than Bolt," Deej said. "The guy was just not cool."

"But he was world champion five times," Calvin argued. "Held world records in the 60 meters and 100 meters at the same time. He's the only sprinter who ever did that."

"You just like him 'cause you both have the same build and you have kinda the same running style. But you gotta admit it, Calvin. Maurice Greene wins the prize for bein' cocky. Go on. Tell her."

Calvin shrugged. "Okay. There was this race in '04. Maurice smoked all the other runners, which was pretty much what everybody was expectin'. But guess what he did right after he won?"

"Tell me."

"He took his shoes off and dropped them on the track. And he had set it up before the race that one of his teammates would come out with a fire extinguisher and spray his shoes. It was s'posed to be like they was on fire or somethin', and this guy had to put out the fire. Maurice's shoes was smokin' hot from him runnin' so fast."

Junior laughed. "Okay. I get it. These guys are all show-offs. Now let me see them run."

"Who do you want to see first?" Deej asked. "Bolt or Greene?"

"Show me the one who runs like Calvin."

"I thought you'd say that." Deej clicked the PLAY button on the screen. "Okay. So here's Greene settin' the world record way back in '99."

The race began, and Junior and Calvin both leaned toward the screen.

"See how he keeps his head down at the beginning?" Calvin said. "The other runners are runnin' straight up already, but he's still got his head low. That helps him pick up speed. It's called the drive phase." Calvin got excited and leaned closer. "See? He's already out in front. And he's stayin' long and relaxed. The others are slowin' down and...damn, he crossed the finish line already." Calvin sat back again. "He ran that race in 9.79 seconds."

"It's over so fast!" Junior said.

"That's why the start and the drive are so important. Then in the middle of the race you keep your stride long by lifting your knees high. And you try and stay relaxed. The more relaxed you are, the faster you'll be."

"Can you show me again?" Junior asked. "This time, pause it so I can see what you're talking about. And explain to me how you can stay relaxed in the middle of a race."

Deej stood up and handed the laptop to Junior. "And don't forget to watch that little show he put on with those smokin' hot shoes."

"You leavin' now?" Calvin asked.

"I'd like to keep sittin' on the couch between you two lovebirds, but the educational part of my evening is now over. Gotta bounce. See you-all later."

9

**Junior cared a lot about school, so Calvin tried to keep a positive** attitude too. He even did his homework sometimes and was surprised at how much of a difference it made in his grades. But after a while HT started wearing him down.

Calvin's school was so different from Junior's, they could have been on different planets instead of just a few blocks apart. His school wasn't clean and safe, with decent sports equipment and enough books for every student. At HT, everything, including most of the staff, was old, worn out, or just not very good to start with. So a lot of kids didn't bother coming after the first few weeks.

For the kids that did show up, the scene outside the school in the mornings was pretty much the same every day. The dealers and potheads huddled behind the bleachers, taking care of business. All the other kids were out in the open, each person hanging with a certain group. There were jocks, gays, Goths, emos, bangers, techies, skaters. Even some preps, just about the only ones that actually carried books. There were groups no one had thought of a name for yet. One thing you could say for Harry Truman High School, it had diversity with a capital D.

Every morning Calvin and Deej liked to kick it with their boys across the street from the school's front steps. This was prime real estate, and they claimed it on the first day. They were seniors now. By the time you were eighteen, there was nothing illegal about having a cigarette, even though smoking wasn't allowed on school property. Calvin never took more than two quick drags anyway because of being a sprinter. Mostly he just liked hanging with his boys.

One Wednesday morning near the end of October, they finished their smokes and headed inside. As Calvin and Deej waited to go through the metal detector, Mr. Kazinsky, one of the assistant principals, said in a loud voice, "You boys smell like reefer!"

Calvin laughed. He thought it was a joke. No one said "reefer" anymore. Besides, he always got along okay with Kazinsky. The dude was bald and sixty pounds overweight, but he used to be a decent 800-meter distance runner. Back in the day. Whenever they passed each other in the hall, Kazinsky always asked Calvin how track was going.

So Calvin didn't understand what was happening now because he could tell by Kazinsky's face that he wasn't kidding around. And the next thing he knew, Kazinsky was walking him and Deej down the hall to Principal Nurch's office.

Deej whispered, "Hey, Calvin. I thought you and Kazinsky were cool."

"Me too."

Calvin turned around and looked at Kazinsky with his eyebrows raised, like he was asking him what was going on. But Kazinsky stared straight ahead and wouldn't make eye contact.

When they got to the office, Kazinsky told them to wait and went in alone to see Nurch. After a minute, Kazinsky opened the door and told Calvin and Deej to go in. He followed them, closed the door, and stood in front of it, arms folded on top of his gut.

Nurch looked up from some papers on his desk. "What have you two got to say for yourselves?"

"We didn't do anything," Calvin answered.

Nurch spread his hands and tapped his fingertips together. "As I've explained to Assistant Principal Kazinsky, I intend to make some changes here at Harry Truman High School. Discipline has been lax. Students are going to have to learn that, from now on, school rules will be strictly enforced."

"We were just havin' a cigarette," Deej said. "That's all."

"I'm sure Mr. Kazinsky has sufficient grounds for his accusation."

"What's he accusing us of?" Calvin asked.

"Possession and use of illegal substances," Nurch answered.

"That's not true!" Deej said. "And he knows it."

Calvin tried looking at Kazinsky again, but he stood by the door with his face like a stone.

"Mr. Kazinsky, I authorize you to search these boys' lockers."

"Good idea!" Deej yelled.

"Don't get hostile, Mr. Johnson," Nurch said to Deej. "It's not in your best interest. Believe me."

On the way to the lockers, Kazinsky still refused to look at Calvin or Deej, and he wouldn't answer any questions. It was like the man had suddenly gone deaf.

They reached Calvin's locker first. Kazinsky opened it, pulled everything out, and dumped it on the floor. Books, binders, loose papers, clothes, food, lighter, sneakers, basketball. Deej had the same, plus cigarettes and a bottle of aspirin because he got bad headaches sometimes.

The search was still going on when the bell rang at the end of first period. Kids spilled into the hall, walking around the three of them standing by Deej's locker with his stuff all over the floor. The kids passed slowly, staring and whispering.

Kazinsky snapped, "Get to class!" and then walked Calvin and Deej back to the office. He put what he'd found on the principal's desk. A lighter, some cigarettes, the aspirin. That was all.

"I told you," Calvin said. "We aren't stoners. Me and Deej don't bring drugs to school."

Nurch ignored him and said, "Empty your pockets. Both of you."

Calvin started to do it, but Deej said, "Don't," in a voice that was more like a dog growling than any sound you'd expect a person to make.

They all stood there for a few seconds, nobody saying anything.

Finally Calvin said, real quiet, "Come on, Deej. It's easier just to do what they say. Get this over with."

Deej shook his head. "No. Don't you see how totally wack this is?" He narrowed his eyes at Kazinsky. "Calvin here has been on the track team three years. Worked hard. He says you even talk to him about running sometimes. Turns out you don't even care about that, do you?"

Kazinsky didn't answer.

Nurch said, "I'm suspending you both for a week."

Deej snarled, "I'm not finished yet. In three years, me and Calvin never got in any trouble. Do you know how hard that is? But we done it. We see somethin' bad goin' down? Somethin' bad that's about to happen? Maybe some brothers gettin' ready to mix it up in the lunchroom? We just walk away. Don't even stick around to watch. Now we find out, it don't make no difference. We tell you we don't have weed, and you won't believe us. You people make me sick."

"Are you finished?" Nurch asked. "Because if you're not going to show me what's in your pockets, you're suspended."

Deej didn't answer. Calvin looked over at him. He could tell there was no way Deej was backing down on this. There was just one problem.

Calvin looked at Nurch and asked, "If I get suspended, can I still run in the District Championship?"

It was Kazinsky who answered, his eyes flicking in Calvin's direction but not actually looking at him. "The track championship is in May. If you don't make any trouble next semester, you'll be eligible to compete."

"I'm offering you boys one last chance to turn out your pockets," Nurch said.

Calvin's jaw tightened. He looked at Deej again. Deej stared straight ahead.

"Get out of here. Both of you," Nurch said.

Deej walked to the door and yanked it open. "C'mon, Calvin. Let's blow this joint."

10

**Momma was upset. "Why didn't you and Deej empty your pockets** like they asked?"

"They'd already made up their minds to kick us out."

"You don't know that."

"Kazinsky must be trying to impress the new principal. Show how tough he is."

"A one-week suspension! That looks bad on your record, Calvin. What about keeping up with your schoolwork? And what will Coach Wilson and Albert say?"

"Coach Wilson has jury duty. Been out the whole week. But even Kazinksy says I can still run in the championship. I asked about it."

After they'd walked out of school that morning, Deej wanted Calvin to hang out for a while. Get something to eat. Deej was still worked up and wanted to talk about what happened. He was proud they had stood up for themselves, thought it was all good.

What Calvin wanted was to go over to Nail Magick and tell Momma what happened, get it over with. Instead of worrying all day about what she'd say. How she'd look.

But now that he'd told her, now that they were sitting face to face in the empty shop, Calvin was hoping a customer would walk in. Give him an excuse to stand up and walk out the door. He wanted to leave. But he knew he couldn't. Not until Momma had her say.

"Don't you see, Calvin? That new principal. Mr. Nurch is his name? He doesn't know you. He's going to think you're a troublemaker."

"The secretary gave me a paper. Says you gotta go for a conference. You gotta call for an appointment."

"Where is it?"

Calvin dug the folded-up paper out of his jeans and handed it to her.

Momma opened the paper and smoothed it out. She read it over carefully and sighed.

"I'm sorry," Calvin said, meaning it.

"It's not just me you should be sorry about. You let yourself down too. And Little Lewis. And Junior. Albert. Coach Wilson. All the people who care about you."

Calvin slouched lower in his chair. "Junior's gonna be upset." He paused. "So's her daddy." He stared at his feet, shaking his head. "Guess I blew it."

Calvin was mixed up. Back in Nurch's office, when he and Deej stood up for themselves, it seemed like the right thing to do. It seemed important not to let themselves get pushed around. Maybe it was a little risky, but it was worth it. And when Kazinsky said Calvin could still run in the spring, it seemed like there wasn't even much risk.

Plus it was righteous hearing Deej say how unfair it was for them to be punished over something they didn't even do. How they'd never been in trouble before, and that should count for something. Calvin had actually imagined Junior being proud of him when he told her about it.

But now he was thinking maybe he'd been stupid to go along with Deej. Maybe Calvin was going to end up paying for it in a lot of small ways he didn't even know about yet. It wasn't the same for Deej. The only person who cared what Deej did was Granny Henry. And she barely knew what Deej was up to half the time. But things were different for Calvin. He should be smart enough to know that.

"Calvin, are you listening to me?" Momma was shaking her finger at him. "Make sure this suspension doesn't start you down a bad road. Do you understand me? No more trouble. You've got too much to lose. If you don't graduate, it will break my heart. I'm telling you that right now. And if you don't get to race in that championship, it will break your heart. And mine. Plus a whole lot of other folks'."

A customer walked in. It was Mrs. Asamowei, one of Momma's regulars.

"Is that you, Calvin? What are you doing here, child? You haven't dropped out of school, have you?"

"No, he hasn't," Momma answered. "He's here to clean up my stockroom. He's going to start by taking everything off the shelves. Then he's going to wipe them down. Then he's going to put everything back on the shelves. After that he'll get a broom and sweep out the place. And then I'll find some boxes for him to unpack."

Mrs. Asamowei smiled widely and patted her fancy Nigerian head wrap. "That's right, Ruby," she said to Momma. "Keep the children busy. Then maybe you can keep them safe."

That afternoon, Calvin didn't get to meet Junior after school because Momma kept finding jobs for him at the shop. The whole time he was working, he was checking the clock on the wall, so he could call Junior as soon as her school let out. He imagined her standing in front of Saint Bernadette's with her friends. He pictured her looking around, expecting to see him come jogging around the corner.

Finally the clock said three. Calvin gave Junior five minutes to get outside of the building, and then he called.

Right away he told her about getting suspended. His heart kind of rolled over when he heard how upset she was.

"We weren't doing anything wrong, Junior. All we did was refuse to show them what was in our pockets. And then Deej mouthed off some."

"Why didn't you show them? Since you didn't have any drugs on you?"

"We were both mad. We never get into trouble. They shoulda believed us."

"Didn't you try talking to them?"

"They wouldn't listen."

"I don't get it. Why would they just kick you out?"

"It's not like Saint B's. At HT, they kick kids out all the time. Usually it's for something real. Last week there were girl gangs goin' at it in the gym. But it doesn't have to be real. It can be somethin' they just make up. They never bother to find out what's really goin' on."

"But you and Deej were innocent!"

"They don't care!" Calvin said, raising his voice. He forced himself to calm down. "You're right about one thing, though. If we'd showed them we didn't have anything on us, it might have gone down different. We were stupid."

"I feel so bad for you, baby. They shouldn't have treated you like that." It was like she was touching him with her voice.

"Junior, do you think maybe I could see you tonight? Just this once?"

"I'll ask Daddy and call you back."

"Okay. I gotta go to Albert's now. You can call me there. I'll keep my cell on."

11

**After he got home from work, Calvin rushed through dinner and** then told Momma he was going to Junior's. "Her daddy said we could sit on the porch for a while."

"Do you want the car?"

"Nah, I'd rather run."

Calvin went north on Georgia Avenue at an easy jog. Usually when he ran, he just did it. But there were other times, like now, when for some reason he would be aware of every muscle in his body. And he would be amazed at how easy running was for him, how it seemed like something he was born to do.

He loved everything about running. Loved feeling his knee lift, his leg reach out, his foot roll down and flex as his weight shifted forward, his calf tighten as he pushed off for the next stride. It was simple and easy. The same motion repeated thousands of times. He understood it in a way he didn't understand a lot of other things. It made sense to him. And when he ran, somehow the world made sense too.

After about a quarter mile, he turned and ran west until he got to Junior's street. Most of the houses here had real lawns, and bushes that somebody bothered to trim. Or a small tree with a circle of white-painted rocks around it. A few blocks made a big difference in this part of the city.

Junior was on the lookout so Calvin wouldn't have to come inside. As he ran up the porch steps, he saw the curtains move at the living room window. Next thing he knew, Junior was outside and in his arms.

"You got here fast. Did you run the whole way?"

"I jogged."

"You're not even out of breath."

"Running's what I'm good at. You know that."

"You're good at other things too, Calvin."

"Yeah? Like what?"

"You're good-looking. And you're very strong. You have these amazing muscles." Junior stroked his chest through his T-shirt, then turned her face up and kissed him. He kissed her back, hungrily. "And you're a great kisser," she murmured.

Calvin squinted up at the light over the front door. "Do you think we could turn that off?"

"I already tried. Daddy put it back on." Junior pulled Calvin over to a double rocker that sat in a corner of the porch. "C'mon. It's darker over here."

They kissed again. It went on for a while. When they finally stopped, both of them were breathing hard.

"We better slow down," Junior said, pushing away from him with a shaky laugh.

Calvin's voice was almost a groan as he said, "Sometimes I wish we could—you know."

She nodded. "Me too."

Calvin stood up and went to lean against the porch railing. "I think I should stay over here for a while."

Junior giggled and straightened her fuzzy white sweater. Neither of them said anything.

Finally Junior spoke. "Daddy was upset when I told him what happened to you and Deej."

"Why'd you tell him?"

"I had to. He'd find out anyway. Daddy knows a lot of people."

"Does he know me and Deej are innocent?"

"I told him that. He blames the whole thing on Deej." Junior sat up tall and imitated her father's deep voice. "That Deej is trouble."

"It's not true."

"I know it's not. But that's what Daddy says."

Calvin pushed himself off the railing. "Try to make him understand, okay? Me and Deej were innocent. They wouldn't listen. Deej did sorta go off on them, but he was right. When I found out I could still be in the championship, I backed him up. Like he always does for me. Maybe it wasn't the smartest thing I ever did, but it wasn't wrong. What they did was wrong. What we did was just stupid."

"Okay, okay," Junior said softly. "I believe you, Calvin."

She patted the space beside her. Calvin sat back down, and Junior snuggled against his chest. He pushed the rocker as he stroked her hair.

"Did I ever tell you how me and Deej met?" Calvin asked.

Junior shook her head.

"Daddy Lewis and Momma had split up for a while. Little Lewis wasn't born yet. It was a bad time. We didn't have much money. Momma was working for somebody else, so she had to put me in daycare. She thought the place was okay. But the big kids beat up on the little kids. And I was one of the little kids. My stomach was in knots every day 'cause of that place."

"That's terrible," Junior whispered.

"Then Deej showed up. He was little too. But he wasn't scared. He showed me how to stand up for myself. Me and Deej stuck together. And after a while the big kids left us alone."

"He's always been there for you."

"Yeah." Calvin's voice sounded far away. Then he shook himself and said, "Let's stop bein' so serious. C'mon, Junior. You gotta cheer me up."

Their kiss was interrupted when the porch light switched off and on and the door opened.

"Good evening, Calvin," Junior's father said.

Calvin jumped to his feet. "Good evening, sir."

"Carla told me what happened today. I have to say I was disappointed, Calvin. But I'm giving you a second chance. There are two reasons. One is that Carla is fond of you. The more important reason is that I know you treat her with the respect she deserves. However, I want to make it very clear that I won't have my only daughter spending time with a young man who gets into this kind of trouble. Don't let anything like this happen again."

"Yes, sir."

"Carla has to come inside now. Unlike you, she has school tomorrow."

Junior's kiss brushed Calvin's cheek and saved him from having to think of something to say. "Sorry," she whispered. "Call me later, okay?"

Calvin nodded and stepped off the porch. Junior followed her father inside and closed the door.

Calvin turned toward home, but then he realized it was the last place he wanted to be. He was all wound up inside. Being with Junior. Getting kicked out of school. He felt ready to explode. He needed to run. Run hard. Maybe he'd call Deej and see if he could help Calvin work out.

He was reaching for his cell phone when it rang.

"Hey, bro," Deej said. "Where you at?"

"Just saw Junior. Had to tell her about me and you gettin' thrown out of school."

"How'd she take it?"

"She was cool, once I explained how it all went down."

"Her daddy know?"

"Yeah. After my ten minutes was up, he came out and glared at me. Then gave me a whatchacallit, a ultimatum, 'bout how he was gonna let me keep seein' Junior but I better not mess up again."

"Man! I know how much you like Junior and all, but are you sure she's worth it? I mean, you and her ain't even doin' it, and you still gotta worry 'bout her daddy buttin' in. This thing that happened at school, what business is it of his? Who put him in charge?"

"She is worth it, Deej. To me, anyway. You know I love everything 'bout that girl."

"Okay then. Long as you're sure. Listen, I'm not doin' nothin' right now. You up for workin' out?"

"Yeah. I was gonna call you. I need to go home first. Get my stuff."

"Nah. Meet me at school. I'll borrow Danette's car, drive by your place, and get what you need. Just shoes and shorts, right? You can change in the car."

As he headed toward school, Calvin could already feel himself starting to relax. He loved the track late at night. Loved having the place to himself. Deej being there with him was as good as being alone. Better. It was being alone without being lonely.

12

**The next day when Calvin showed up for work, he found Albert**
in the back room pouring water into the coffeemaker. Albert looked
around, surprised to see him.

"What are you doing here, Calvin? Do you have a day off from
school?"

"No. I got kicked out. For one week. Me and Deej both."

"You got suspended? When did this happen?"

"Yesterday."

"I don't understand. This happened yesterday?" Albert pressed
the START button on the machine and turned to face Calvin. "You came
to work yesterday and you didn't say anything. Why didn't you tell me
then?"

Calvin shrugged.

"Something like this happens, Calvin, I want to know about it.
There's trust involved here."

"I was sick of talkin' about it. First Deej was all worked up and
wanted to talk about it. Then I had to tell Momma. And she wanted
to talk about it. Then Junior wanted to talk about it. By the time I got
here yesterday, I didn't even want to think about it. I wasn't keepin' it
from you. I just figured I'd tell you today, that's all."

"I assume you're here early because you want to work?"

"Yeah. I mean, if it's okay with you."

"It's fine. But don't you see that it would have been good for
you to give me some notice? I could have planned for you being
here. This way, I only have one car for you to detail, so I can't use
you the whole day. Now that I know you'll be around, I'll call back
some customers who asked for appointments. You can work full days
starting tomorrow."

"Thanks, Albert."

"You did say you were suspended for a whole week? Five
days?"

"That's right."

"That's a lot of school to miss." Albert sighed and shook his
head. "We need to talk, Calvin. I was going to make those calls right

48

now. But they can wait. Come into my office for a minute. I want you to sit down and tell me what happened."

Calvin followed Albert into his office and told the whole story one more time.

When he was finished, Albert said, "Let's see if I've got this straight. You didn't have any drugs on you, but you wouldn't prove it by showing them what was in your pockets. Deej got angry and said some things he shouldn't have. And you backed him up. That's what got you thrown out?"

"That's about right."

Albert frowned. "Sounds like Deej put you in a bad spot, Calvin. He lost his temper. Maybe he had reason to. But he wasn't risking much. Just being thrown out, which he probably doesn't mind. You were the one with something to lose—your eligibility for the championship. I'm surprised Deej would do that to you."

"I guess Deej wasn't thinkin' 'bout all that when he was yellin' at Nurch. He just kinda lost his head. He can be like that."

"This kind of thing worries me, Calvin. It's not right when a good kid like you gets suspended. I'm glad to hear you're not going to lose your eligibility. But you're still going to miss an entire week of school. You'll have extra work to do. Tests to make up. It'll be harder to keep your grades up. Harder to graduate."

Calvin stared at the neat piles of papers on Albert's desk. "I guess I could go get my stuff out of my locker. Ask Junior to help me some."

"That's a good idea. But, more important, what are you going to do about Deej?"

"Whadya mean?"

"Here's a question for you, Calvin. Would you have shown Mr. Nurch what you had in your pockets if you'd been in his office by yourself?"

Calvin thought back. "I think so. I was pretty ready to go along with what he wanted."

"But Deej decided to make a stand, and so you went along with Deej instead. Is that it?"

"I guess."

"Deej made a stand and you backed him up. Because you're friends."

"What's wrong with that?"

Albert sighed. "I like Deej. He's basically a good kid. I know you two have been friends a long time. But Deej is cocky. He's not as smart as he thinks he is. I'm afraid that one of these days he's going to get himself into trouble. And you too, if you're not careful."

"Albert, can I ask you a favor? Can we not talk about this anymore? I been talkin' so much since yesterday, I feel like my head's gonna explode."

Albert nodded and reached for the phone. "Sure, Calvin. We're done. But think about what I said, will you?"

Once he started working, Calvin felt better. His headache went away. It seemed like the soapy sponge in his hand wasn't just cleaning the car, it was washing out his brain too. What happened yesterday wasn't such a big deal. Everyone was making it into more than what it was. He didn't want to have to think about it anymore. He just wanted to use the hose and wash it all away. Maybe he'd think about some of this stuff later.

Calvin worked through lunch and was finished by one. Then he took Zipper for his walk, and afterward he sat with him out in the car yard, and they played tug-of-war. Sometimes Calvin wished he had a dog. Dogs were great when you were feeling down. Dogs were always happy to be with you, no matter what. Dogs didn't talk.

Calvin was putting Zipper back in his crate when Albert stuck his head in the room.

Calvin was surprised to see him smiling.

"You almost done, Calvin?"

"Uh-huh."

"I'm thinking I might finish early too. How about if you meet me at the track at four? I have something to show you."

"Okay. Sure."

So at four, Calvin was jogging around the track, starting to feel pretty good, when Albert walked up carrying a big cardboard shipping box.

Calvin trotted over. "What you got there?"

Albert didn't say anything. He put the carton on the ground. The address of an athletic supplier was printed on the outside.

"Let me say something first, Calvin. I'm still unhappy about your suspension. I want you to be clear on that. What's in the box is something I ordered a few months ago, but it didn't come until today. Maybe that's a good thing. This is most definitely not a reward. I want you to think of it as a reminder."

"A reminder of what?"

"A reminder of how hard you've worked and how fast you can be. Let me ask you something, Calvin. You've been to a lot of track meets. How many times have you seen a really good relay team mess up the baton pass? Ten? Twenty?"

"Somethin' like that. It happens a lot."

"Why?"

"Somebody's not paying attention. They're overconfident. They forget to keep their head in the race."

"Exactly. You have a goal for yourself. To win the 100-meter dash at the District Championship. It's a worthy goal, Calvin. Worthy of the effort it takes. Don't get distracted. Don't forget what it is you want. When you were in Principal Nurch's office and you risked your dream, you let yourself get distracted. Don't do that to yourself."

"Okay."

"Right. No more speeches. I know you're sick of them. Go ahead, Calvin. Open the box."

There were two small boxes inside the big one. Both the same.

"Sweet!" Calvin said, opening one of the boxes and unwrapping what was inside. It was a starting block, the latest model, basically a piece of metal with two adjustable footplates attached. Starting blocks were for pushing off at the start of a race.

Albert had him turn the block over so they could admire it from all sides. "See? This is how you adjust the space between the footplates. We'll figure out the best distance to help you get maximum acceleration."

"Man, we really needed these. Those starting blocks we been usin' are complete crap. How'd you get the school to spring for new ones?"

"They didn't," Albert said. "I did."

"You're kiddin' me! They cost about a hundred each."

"More than that," Albert said. "But the school's starting blocks are almost twenty years old. They're junk. Last year I checked out what the other teams use. The good teams. Then I got the same thing for us."

"Does Coach Wilson know about this?"

"Of course. We talked about how there are some really good runners on the team this year. So now is the time to get new blocks. When he told me there wasn't enough money in the athletic budget, I said I'd pay for them."

Calvin looked at Albert and shook his head. "I can't believe you spent your own money that way."

"You've only got one chance at this, Calvin. To be the best." Calvin nodded.

"But new blocks are just the beginning. You've got to stay focused. Have you and Deej been sticking to the workout schedule I gave you?"

"Yeah. We added a couple new drills we found online, but remember you and me talked about it, and you said it was okay."

Albert handed Calvin the blocks. "You go nail these down on the track nice and tight, and we'll start trying to figure out the best way to adjust them for you. It's going to take a couple of sessions before we get them just right. Maybe even a few weeks. But we know they're going to help you."

Walking home from the track, Calvin felt all right. Better than all right. He felt good. His head was clear again. He had his bounce back. He could feel it in his knees.

When he got close to his street, a car came around the corner real fast. It was a silver Ford Explorer like the one Norris drove. As the car sped past, Calvin recognized Norris in the back seat with a couple of girls. Deej was driving.

13

**The next day Calvin put in nine hours working for Albert, but he still** called Deej maybe twenty times. He wanted to know where Deej was. Wanted to know if he was with Norris.

Finally Deej called him.

"Hey, man!" Calvin said. "I been leavin' you messages."

"I called you too," Deej said. "Last night. Where was you at?"

"Momma had me workin' late. Doin' stuff at the shop."

"Too bad. I was callin' to find out was you up for meetin' Cousin Norris."

"What?"

"I was out with Cousin Norris last night. Thought you might wanna come with us."

"What're you talkin' 'bout, Deej? This is the dude that wants to break my knees. Remember?"

"Course I remember. But I was thinkin' maybe if you two spent some time together, got to know each other, then maybe he wouldn't feel that way so much. Might be a smart thing to do."

"You told me yourself that Norris P is vicious. You said I should stay away from him."

"Maybe I was wrong."

"How can you be wrong 'bout somethin' like that?"

"He's not that bad when you spend time with him."

"I don't wanna spend time with him."

"That's cool. Just thought I'd ask, is all."

"Let's talk 'bout somethin' else."

"Okay." Deej paused. "So tell me how you're fixed for money these days."

"I'm workin' extra for Albert, so my cash is flowin' pretty good. I can give you some if you need it."

"No way, man. I went to Charles Town Races today, over in West Virginia. Played the ponies. I'm up six hundred."

"Who were you with, Deej?"

"How 'bout we take the girls out tomorrow night? You and Junior. Me and Tonya. We can double-date and celebrate."

"You got somethin' in mind?" Calvin asked.

"That fancy Mexican place. Rio Something."

"You sure you want Mexican?"

"This place is nice. I been there. The girls'll dig it. Plus I know a waiter there. He'll serve us all drinks. Junior too, if you want."

"Nah. I don't want her to get messed up. I'm on thin ice with her daddy already. The rest sounds good, though. I'll let her know."

Saturday night started out fun. The girls looked fine. Tonya was wearing something tight and red and shiny. Junior's dress was gold and shimmery. She wore the beaded earrings from the night she and Calvin met. She knew he liked them.

There were two musicians in big sparkly hats walking around the restaurant. They stopped at every table and played loud Mexican music for tips. Deej and Calvin said it sounded awful, but the girls liked it.

Since Junior wasn't drinking, Calvin just had two beers. It was still fun, though. They ate and drank and talked and laughed, all squeezed together in a padded booth.

Around the time they were ready to order dessert, Calvin asked Deej about winning on the horses at Charles Town.

"How'd you do it? 'Cause when you and me went that time, we never won more'n a few bucks."

"That's 'cause we just bet on a horse if it looked fast. Or if we liked the name. You gotta be scientific."

"Like how?" Tonya wanted to know.

"The main thing is to study the racing form. Know how the horse is runnin'. Who he's up against. Maybe know somethin' 'bout the jockey and trainer."

"How'd you learn all that in just one day?" Junior asked.

Calvin spoke up. "I'm guessin' his cousin was showin' him. Isn't that right, Deej?"

Tonya leaned across the table toward Junior and said in a loud whisper, "You know about Deej's cousin, don't you?"

"I guess not."

"Deej is cousins with Norris Palmer," Tonya said.

"You mean the guy that's always mixed up in a lot of bad stuff you see on the news?" Junior asked.

Tonya nodded. "That's Deej's cousin." She seemed to enjoy the shock on Junior's face.

"Be quiet, Tonya," Deej said. "Drink your drink."

Junior turned to Calvin. "Did you know Deej's cousin is Norris Palmer?" she asked.

"Yeah. I knew. Keep your voice down, Junior, okay?"

Nobody said anything.

Finally Deej spoke. "We gonna order dessert now, or what?"

Later that night, after he took Junior home, Calvin called Deej. "So what were we gonna do the other night when you wanted me to go out with you and Norris P?"

"We were headed to a street race. Out in Prince George's County."

"Yeah, I heard that's somethin' they like out in P.G. Don't people get killed doin' that?"

"Nah. Once in a while a car goes off the road. But the driver usually just walks away. It's fun to watch. There's this dark stretch of road that's way out in the country. It's maybe a mile long and real straight. There's nothin' on it, no houses or stores or anything. With their lights on, you can see the cars comin' from far away. And they come closer and closer, and you start to hear the engines screamin'. And then they're going by at maybe a hundred miles an hour. And all around you it's just noise and air pushin' against you. Could be a tornado or somethin'. It's a rush. Like a video game."

"Only real," Calvin said.

"Yeah. So it's better."

"How many people come out to watch one of these things?"

"Maybe a hundred. Maybe more. Afterward people turn on their car lights and their stereos and everybody dances in the street. It's cool. Like a party. You'd like it."

"Maybe."

"The whole scene is amazing. I really dig it. You would too, Calvin."

"That rush you're talkin' about—that's how I feel when I run."

"See? I can't run. But I gotta get that feelin' somehow. Everybody does."

On Sunday, Calvin didn't see Deej or even talk to him. But he thought about him all the time. He worried what Deej might be up to. But he was also mad at him for being stupid.

It was boring not having Deej to hang out with, so Calvin offered to play ball with Little Lewis. On their way to the school, he noticed his brother trying to carry the basketball wedged between his elbow and hip in that cool way ballers do. But his arms were too short. There was a time Calvin would've teased Lewis about this. Instead he said, "So, little brother, what you wanna work on?"

"Shooting! What else is there?"

"Plenty. You gotta learn to keep the ball when somebody wants to take it off you. Wait till you're bigger to work on your shot. Otherwise all you'll do is mess up your form."

"You sayin' my form's good, Calvin?"

"Not bad. Your shot's got a decent arc. Wait a while yet. You grow a few more inches, it'll all come together."

"I'm tired of waitin' for stuff."

"Waitin's hard. But everybody's gotta do it. Look at me. I'm waitin' for track season to start in the spring. Waitin' to run in the championship. Waitin' to graduate. Life's full of waitin'."

Little Lewis was listening hard, taking in every word Calvin said. "Kids have to wait lots more'n grownups. It's not fair."

Calvin stopped walking. "Little Lewis, you just said somethin' real smart."

"What?"

"Sit down here on the curb for a minute."

"But the court's right over there!"

Calvin ignored him and sat down, trying to figure out his idea before it got away from him.

"The reason kids gotta wait more'n grownups is 'cause when you're a kid, you still have lotsa things ahead of you. Lotsa things comin' up. And that's good."

"If you say so."

"Sure it is. You've seen the drunks sleepin' in the doorways up on Georgia Avenue, right?"

Little Lewis nodded.

"They don't have anything ahead of 'em. They know it, too. That's why they're drunk all the time. Can't stand the thought that all the good stuff's behind them."

"So I should be happy I gotta wait for things?"

"Yeah. I guess so."

They sat for a minute. Then Little Lewis jumped up and said, "Can we play now? Or do I have to wait for that too?"

Calvin grabbed the ball from him and ran onto the court. "Okay, Shorty. Show me what you got."

"Don't call me Shorty!" Little Lewis roared. He threw himself at Calvin and managed to get the ball back. He danced off with it, laughing. Then he dribbled in close. "Calvin, you talk like a old man. I'm thinkin' you're too old and worn out to play with me. C'mon. Try and take the ball." Finally Little Lewis was working on his ball handling.

On the way home they stopped at Popeye's and picked up chicken and biscuits for dinner. Momma was off at somebody's daughter's baby shower. Calvin and Little Lewis ate in the living room and watched wrestling on TV.

14

**After their suspension ended, Calvin tried to get Deej to go back to** HT with him, but Deej wouldn't do it. He was still mad about getting kicked out.

Calvin missed hanging with Deej every morning before school, missed talking to him about the crazy place HT was. But Deej wasn't interested.

Then Deej called one night while Calvin was doing bench presses in the basement. Calvin picked up right away.

"What's goin' on?" Deej asked.

"Not much. What's goin' on with you?"

"Everything's cool."

"You okay, Deej? You don't sound right."

"I told you. It's all good."

"It ain't all good, Deej. I can tell."

A long pause. Then Deej's voice, talking low. "I'm in trouble, Calvin."

"What kinda trouble?"

"All kinds."

"Okay, what's the first trouble?"

"I dropped fifteen hundred on the ponies."

"You said you had it all figured out."

"That's what I thought. Didn't think I could lose like that. Not over and over."

"Lemme guess. Norris P gave you money."

"That's right. But he says I don't have to pay him back."

Calvin thought about that for a while. "What's he want you to do, Deej?"

Calvin could hear his friend breathing short and fast, like somebody scared. Calvin had never heard Deej sound scared before.

"Or did you do it already?"

Silence.

Calvin tried to stay calm. "Whadya do?"

Deej's answer was so quiet, Calvin couldn't hear it.

"Where are you, Deej?"

"My basement."

"Meet me at school. On the track. Ten minutes."

When Calvin got to the track, Deej was already there. But Calvin didn't see him right away. Deej was sitting in the bleachers, about halfway up, smoking a cigarette. His hand was the only thing that moved. The rest of him was completely still, like he was trying to be invisible.

Calvin climbed up the steps and sat down. Deej offered to share his cigarette, but Calvin waved it off. Neither of them spoke. Deej finished and flicked the butt into the distance. Calvin watched the lit end flare before it disappeared into the blackness of the bleachers.

"So tell me. What went down with Norris P?"

"I boosted a car for him last night. He had a buyer all lined up for it. In Virginia."

"Aw, Deej. Why'd you have to go and do that?"

"It's complicated."

Calvin waited for Deej to say more, but he didn't.

Finally Calvin asked, "You do the job alone?"

"Yeah. Just me."

"So if the cops find the car, nothin' can be traced to Norris P 'cause he didn't do it."

"That's right," Deej said.

"You're one of his boys, aren't you?"

"I been one of his boys for a while now."

Calvin didn't say anything. Just stared off into the dark, thinking.

"What else you done?"

"Carryin' stuff. Drugs. Money. Cousin Norris has me doing some protection stuff. Like what he did with your momma. So far I been lucky. People paid me without me havin' to do nothin'."

"Christ, Deej! How'd you get in so deep with Norris P? You said you was just doin' little jobs for him. You made it sound like it was no big deal."

"The thing is, Calvin, most of the time I like hangin' with Cousin Norris."

"I'm startin' to figure that out. What I still don't get is why." 59

"I dunno. I guess 'cause he gets me to do stuff I know I shouldn't. It makes me feel one hundred percent alive. I like that feelin', Calvin. I really do. It's like I'm addicted to it or somethin'."

"But now you're worried."

"This is the first time I stole somethin' on my own. All the other times, I was just, you know, helpin' Norris's boys. I wasn't the main guy doin' it. This time I was. It's all happenin' too fast, Calvin. You know? I need things to slow down. I feel like I'm gettin' in too deep. I didn't think that'd happen. Thought I was too smart."

"We gotta get you outta this, Deej."

15

**After that it got hard for Calvin to find out just what Deej was up to.**
Whenever they talked, Calvin tried asking him what was going on with
Norris. What had happened with the car Deej stole. Whether Deej
was still worried about the other stuff Norris had him doing. But Deej
wouldn't answer any of his questions, so Calvin stopped asking.

Then, right after Thanksgiving, Deej called and said, "Cousin
Norris left town."

"Are you for real?"

"Yeah. Looks like Christmas came early this year."

"Is he comin' back? 'Cause I'd feel better if he was locked up
somewhere."

Deej laughed, a sound Calvin realized he hadn't heard in a
while. "Yeah, that'd be good. But this ain't bad. The boys say he's
gone till after New Year's. Working on a deal up in Atlantic City or
somethin' like that."

"Maybe while he's gone, you can figure out a way to get out
from under him."

"One thing for sure. I'm really gonna enjoy Christmas this year.
To start with, I got plenty of money."

Calvin didn't want to hear about Deej's money. Instead he
asked, "You done any shoppin' yet?"

"Thought I'd start tomorrow. Get somethin' for Danette and
Shania. We ain't that close, on account of we all got different daddies.
But Granny Henry likes it at Christmas when we act like a real family.
And you know how I feel 'bout Granny Henry. She's my Number One
Girl."

"I'm thinkin' of gettin' a cashmere shawl for Momma."

"Something she can wear to church. That's a good idea.
Granny Henry would like that too. Gives her braggin' rights. It's funny
how those ladies like to show theirselves off on a Sunday."

Calvin laughed. "I know what you mean. These nice Christian
ladies gettin' to church early so they can parade around, tryin' to make
each other jealous, sayin' in a loud voice that their boy bought 'em
this or that."

"That's right. So you thought any 'bout what to get Junior?"

"I been thinkin' 'bout it a lot. But I haven't come up with anything yet. All I know is it's gotta be somethin' special."

"Gettin' a present for a girl like that is complicated," Deej said. " 'Cause her daddy's gonna judge you on it."

"She says her daddy likes me again."

"But this is a chance to make him like you more."

"What about a nice watch?"

"Her daddy would go for it. Takes some change. Shows you respect her."

"So that's what I should get?"

"No."

"You just said it was a good idea."

"I said her daddy would like it. But it's like a retirement gift, you know? We can do better."

"I shouldn't buy her clothes. Right?"

"No way. Last thing you want is for her daddy to know you're thinkin' 'bout her body. Hang on a minute. The girls just got home."

Deej covered the phone. It was a while before he came back on. When he did, he said, "Okay, I got it. A leather bag from a good designer. Not a knock-off. The real thing. They said get Coach."

"They both said the same thing?"

"Yeah. They actually agreed on somethin'. Shania said a designer bag. Danette said to buy Coach."

"That's what I should get?"

"Yeah. That's what I'm tellin' you. They said that's what they'd want. It's expensive. Classy. And it won't make Junior's daddy freak."

"Will you come with me to pick it out?"

"Anything to help a brother."

Saturday morning Deej called. "Listen, bro, when you goin' to the mall?"

"This morning. 'Fore it gets crowded."

"You want me to come, you have to go later."

"You're not doin' a job with Norris P's boys, are you?"

"Nothin' like that. Tonya's grandma was comin' up from the

basement with a box full of Christmas stuff. Fell and broke her arm. Got herself pretty banged up. The whole family's at the hospital. Thought I'd stop by and see if Tonya's doin' okay. She and that old lady are real tight."

"You go be with Tonya. If I have trouble makin' up my mind, I'll phone you some pictures. You and Tonya can look at 'em together."

Momma needed the car, so Calvin caught the bus to the mall.

Albert had paid him yesterday, and he was carrying $550 in cash. He could feel the money folded up in the pocket of his jeans, a nice fat wad that made him feel important, successful. He was on his way to a fancy store to buy his girlfriend an expensive Christmas present with money that was all his, and all legal.

Deej had already checked out the prices for him online, so Calvin knew for sure he'd have enough money. It felt good not to have to worry about that. Deej also told him to be sure to hang on to his receipt when he got it. That way Junior could bring the bag back to the store and exchange it if she didn't like what Calvin picked out. So Calvin guessed there really wasn't anything to worry about. Still, he wished Deej was with him.

The bus was standing-room-only by the time it got to the mall, and the big stores were already filling up. Calvin found the Coach store without any trouble. It wasn't crowded at all. There were six bags in the window, each one sitting on its own round stand, like a little throne or something.

Inside were three saleswomen and two customers. All women. All white. Both customers had someone helping them. Calvin walked around the store, picking up bags to get a closer look, checking the prices, waiting for the third saleswoman to come up and offer to help him. She didn't.

He looked over. She saw him looking at her, but she didn't make a move to come and ask if he needed help. She just watched him. In fact, she started following him. Not too close, but close enough to see what he was doing with his hands. He walked over to a rack of wallets and picked one up. It was small enough to slip in his pocket. He glanced over at the woman. She was staring at him with eyes like lasers.

The way she was looking at Calvin made him want to steal something. Or throw something. Or knock over everything in the store. Or just turn around and walk out. But he thought about Junior and how excited she'd be to get a Coach bag. The real thing. He was not leaving this store without Junior's gift.

The youngest saleswoman was ringing up a customer. Calvin walked over to the cash register and waited there with his arms crossed over his chest. The saleswoman looked over at him and smiled. Then she looked past him at the older saleswoman. When she looked back at Calvin, her eyes were big, and Calvin realized she understood exactly what was going on.

She said, "I'll be happy to help you as soon as I finish up here. Would you care to look around?"

"I'll wait till you're done," Calvin said, his jaw clenched from the tension of just standing there when what he really wanted to do was wreck the store.

The saleswoman, whose nametag said Elizabeth, spent a lot of time with Calvin, asking questions about Junior and what colors she liked to wear, showing him different bags and helping him choose the right one. He finally decided on a large shoulder bag made of soft gold leather with a wide strap and lots of chains. It cost four hundred eighty dollars.

Elizabeth rang up the sale, accepted Calvin's cash payment, wrapped the bag in tissue paper, and put it in a fancy Coach gift bag with a big red bow. As she handed the bag to Calvin, she smiled and said, "That's a really nice present. I think your girlfriend will love it."

Calvin thanked her, but he didn't smile back. He knew this Elizabeth was trying hard to be especially nice to him. But it didn't change what that other saleswoman had done. He felt relieved when he could finally walk out of the store.

Afterward, Calvin couldn't get what happened out of his head. Junior's gift sat on his dresser in its fancy bag, and whenever he looked at it he felt bad. Being able to afford a gift like that should have made him feel good. But instead he felt humiliated, like he lost his self-respect. He finally put the bag in his closet. He didn't want to look at it anymore.

It didn't help that he couldn't tell Junior about it. She'd feel bad because it happened when he was buying her present. In the end, her feeling bad about Calvin feeling bad would just add up to more misery.

A few days after it happened, Calvin and Deej were hanging out on a broken-down couch on Deej's front porch. Deej understood exactly how Calvin felt.

"I don't know why it keeps eatin' at me," Calvin said, reaching over and pulling leaves off the dead plants in Granny Henry's window box.

"I do. It's like that time we got thrown out of school. We didn't get suspended because we had weed. We got suspended because they wouldn't believe us when we told them we didn't have weed. It's messed up."

"Yeah," Calvin agreed. "That white bitch in the Coach store just assumed I didn't have enough money. So I had to be there 'cause I was gonna steal somethin'."

Deej lit a cigarette and squinted when the wind blew the smoke into his face. He said, "It was the same thing both times. People wantin' to believe the worst about us."

Calvin nodded. "Except for some reason this feels a lot worse than what happened at school."

"That's 'cause at school we're basically treated like prisoners. They make all the rules and we're s'posed to obey. That's just how it is. We're used to it." Deej took a long drag from his cigarette. "But out in the world, you expect better."

"Especially if you got money in your pocket," Calvin said. "You feel like you're entitled to some respect."

"Uh-huh. And when you get treated like you're a piece of garbage, it makes you wonder what kinda world is out there. Makes you think maybe things ain't never gonna get any better for you."

**Every Christmas, Junior's family went to visit her daddy's people in** South Carolina.

They would be driving down on December 24th. So Calvin and Junior made plans to meet on the 23rd and give each other their presents. Junior was excited when she called that afternoon.

"Our first Christmas, Calvin! Daddy said I could borrow the car. We can drive out to the 'burbs and look at the lights."

"Sounds nice."

"But I have to be back by seven. So we can finish packing and get an early start tomorrow."

"Yeah, Momma wants me home too. She found some more lights for me to put up."

Around four o'clock, Junior pulled up to Calvin's house in her father's gray Lexus SUV. She looked small and cute sitting way up there behind the steering wheel.

Calvin told her to close her eyes so he could put the fancy shopping bag behind the front seat. The bag had the Coach logo all over it, and he didn't want to spoil his big surprise. When it was safely hidden, he slid into the front, leaned over, and kissed her.

"Are you sure you're big enough to be drivin' a car this size?" he asked.

Junior's laugh sounded to Calvin like tiny bells. "I can handle this car, and I can handle you."

"Yes, you can," Calvin agreed.

They drove around, listening to rock'n'roll Christmas songs on an oldies station Junior found. Calvin made a show of being interested in the lights on the houses. But what he liked most was sitting next to Junior. He liked how she reached over and put her hand on his leg whenever they stopped at a light. He liked the sound of her voice and how she always took a little in-breath before she spoke.

"Oooh. Look at that one, Calvin." She pointed to a house with all its trees lit up in blue and green. Giant red-and-white candy canes lined both sides of the front walk. In the middle of the lawn, three reindeer outlined in white lights slowly moved their heads up and down.

"Let's pull over," Calvin said. When Junior had turned off the engine, he asked, "Are you ready for your present?"

Junior nodded.

Calvin watched her face as he reached behind his seat and pulled out the shopping bag covered with pairs of C's facing in different directions.

He laughed softly. "Hey, little girl! You should see how big your eyes are." He handed her the bag. "Go ahead. Open it."

Junior slowly pushed aside layers of tissue paper, glancing up at Calvin and smiling with excitement. When she saw the gold shoulder bag, she let out a little squeal and hugged him.

"Oh, Calvin! It's perfect!"

"Nothin' but the best for my girl."

She pulled it out and held it up, then spent the next few minutes exploring all the chains and straps and buckles.

"How'd you know I always wanted a Coach bag?" she asked, winding her arms around Calvin's neck and giving him a quick kiss. "Okay. Now it's your turn."

Junior turned away, reached into a small gift bag, and took out a box from a fancy jewelry store. Calvin opened it and whistled softly, lifting a heavy silver chain bracelet out of the box.

"Do you like it?" she asked shyly.

"It's beautiful. Just like my girl."

She giggled happily. "Let me put it on you."

They admired their gifts a while longer. Then Calvin pulled Junior onto his lap and wrapped his arms around her.

He felt her weight in his arms and breathed in the smell of her skin and her hair. In the colored glow of the Christmas lights, Calvin held Junior tight.

He wanted them to be together forever.

17

**Right after vacation ended, Deej called Calvin and told him Norris** was back in town.

"You said he was gonna be away for a while."

"It's been a while. One of his boys called me. He got back yesterday."

From then on, Calvin saw less and less of his friend. Deej didn't even pretend to be going to school anymore. Calvin worked out alone now on Tuesdays and Thursdays. Sometimes Deej came by when he was almost finished. But Calvin could tell he was just going through the motions of watching him and giving him encouragement. He wasn't really focused on Calvin. Not like he used to be.

Even when they sat and talked afterward, it wasn't the same. There were too many things Deej wouldn't tell him, things Calvin figured he probably didn't want to know anyway.

Then, one night, Deej called late and woke Calvin up. Deej was breathing funny, and Calvin got ready to hear something bad.

"What's up?" Deej asked.

"Not much. What's up with you?"

"I'm keepin' busy," Deej said.

"Keepin' busy with Norris P?"

"That's right."

Silence.

"Albert still have that watchdog?" Deej asked.

"What? Yeah. His name's Zipper."

"But you and him are friends, right?"

"Uh-huh. Deej, why you callin' so late askin' me 'bout Zipper?"

"And that back room at the shop. The shelves are still full of boxes of junk Albert won't throw out?"

"He doesn't like to get rid of stuff. Says you never know when somethin' might come in handy. Then you'll wish you'd hung on to it."

"I like that. That's good philosophy."

"Is that why you called, Deej? To talk 'bout philosophy?"

"I need a place to put some stuff for a while."

Calvin didn't answer right away. He had a bad feeling. "You should rent one of those storage places, Deej."

"It's only for a week. Cousin Norris says it's up to me to find a place."

"What're you askin'?"

"Cousin Norris thought you could keep the stuff at Albert's. Says it's a chance for you to work off some of your debt. On account of he still owns your knees."

Calvin didn't say anything.

"It's only for a week," Deej repeated.

There was a long silence. Calvin was thinking about when he got kicked out of school and about that white bitch following him in the Coach store. He'd been innocent both times, but it didn't make any difference.

"Calvin? You still there?"

"I'm thinkin'."

"What you thinkin'?"

"Shut up a minute!"

And Calvin thought about all the things Albert had done for him. Helping him run faster. Buying starting blocks. Giving him a job. Trusting him.

"Calvin?"

"Albert's my friend."

"What about me, Calvin? I'm your friend too, ain't I?"

Calvin knew that's what it all came down to, in the end. Albert had been good to Calvin, sure. But Deej was Calvin's oldest, closest friend. Deej understood Calvin like nobody else. Deej was like a brother. Deej was the first person Calvin would go to if he was in trouble. Now he was asking Calvin for help.

"Okay, Deej. I'll do it."

18

**An hour later, Deej drove up to Albert's shop in a mud-brown**
Dodge Caravan with no shine on it anywhere. It was a car no one
would notice. Deej had told him once that Norris had a couple of vans
he called his "utility cars." This must be one of them.

Deej parked the van close to the fence, got out, and opened
the back doors. When Calvin saw the boxes stacked inside, he
froze. Fourteen Blu-ray players in their original boxes. Brand-new.
Unopened.

"Let's get this over with," Deej said.

"Wait a second. You didn't say this stuff was hot."

"Whadya think, Calvin? If it wasn't hot, I could hide it under my
bed."

"But it's all brand-new. It's worth a lotta money. This stuff can
be traced."

"So?"

"Albert will kill me if he finds out. I'll lose my job."

"He'll never know. Trust me."

"But you didn't tell me what it was. You waited till it was too
late for me to change my mind."

"Look, Calvin. I got you out of trouble with Cousin Norris when
he was gonna bust your knees. You owe me. You could say the whole
reason I got involved with Norris is 'cause I was protectin' you."

"You could say that. But it's not true. You were already involved
with Norris P. Remember? You told me you were doin' little jobs for
him. And now the little jobs have turned into you wantin' me to hide
stolen stuff that's brand-new in Albert's shop."

"Cousin Norris wants you involved. He told me. You're puttin'
me in a bad spot if I have to go back and tell him you wouldn't help."

Calvin stood by the van's open door and couldn't think of
anything to say.

"Look. It's no big deal," Deej said. "The stuff'll be gone in a
week. I promise. Albert will never know. We can get away with this. I
know we can."

Calvin slowly nodded, not taking his eyes off the Blu-ray boxes.

Deej grinned and slapped him on the back. "C'mon, bro. Let's do it."

Calvin took a deep breath and nodded again. He wiped his palms on his jeans. He tried not to think about the line he was crossing when he put his hands around the first box and lifted it out.

They worked fast to unload the boxes and stack them by the front door. Then Deej drove down the street and parked the van out of sight while Calvin unlocked the door and started moving the Blu-rays inside.

Deej hurried back and helped Calvin bring in the last of the boxes. Then Calvin locked the front door. Without turning on the lights, they carried the boxes into the back room. Deej had brought flashlights, so they could see enough to arrange the Blu-rays on the shelves, carefully hiding them behind battered cartons of used car parts.

When they were finished, Calvin locked the front door again and looked the place over from the outside to make sure everything seemed normal. Then he walked along the front of the building until he got to the fenced-in car yard, to where Zipper stood looking at him through the heavy chain-link fence.

Zipper hadn't made a sound the whole time Calvin and Deej were carrying boxes into the shop. He'd just stood there watching them.

Calvin had a tuna sandwich with him in case Zipper made any noise. Now he took it out of the wrapper and gave it to him. He didn't crouch down and talk to him like he usually did. He just pushed the halves through the wires and watched Zipper eat them off the oil-stained pavement. Deej stood next to Calvin.

"Not much of a watchdog," Deej said.

"He trusts me. That's all."

Calvin looked at Zipper standing there on the other side of the fence, staring up at him with his foolish tongue hanging sideways out of his mouth.

"Let's get out of here," Calvin said.

• • •

School was a blur the next day. Calvin couldn't think of anything but getting to Albert's to see if everything was cool. He'd already called Junior to tell her he couldn't meet her. He didn't want her around when he was feeling so jumpy. She'd know right away something was up.

When the last bell rang, Calvin had to force himself not to walk to the shop any faster than usual. He didn't want to do anything that would look suspicious.

Then, when he got close, all he wanted to do was turn and run. There was a cop car parked outside the shop.

"Why're the cops here?" Calvin asked Evonne. It was the end of the month, so she was in to work on the accounts.

Calvin tried to sound just normally interested when he asked the question. Not panicked. Not sick at his stomach and ready to throw up.

"Somebody called Albert this morning," Evonne answered. "Said they saw a van parked outside last night. Told Albert he might want to check and see if anything was missing."

"Did Albert look around?"

"Yes."

"Was anything missing?"

"I don't think so."

"So why'd he call the cops?"

"I don't know. Why don't you ask Albert?"

"Did whoever called get a license number or the color of the van?"

Evonne was Albert's niece. Normally she liked talking to Calvin. But now she said, "You got so many questions, go find Albert. I gotta get my work done."

Just then Albert stuck his head out of his office and said, "Calvin, come in here, please."

When Calvin walked into Albert's office, there was a lady cop sitting on the desk. She had one leg hanging over the side, the other planted on the floor. Albert looked at Calvin with an expression on his face that was hard to read.

"What's goin' on?"

"This police officer has some questions for you, Calvin."

"Okay. Sure."

"Do you know an individual by the name of Darryl Johnson, also known as Deej?"

"He's not in trouble, is he?" Calvin knew it was the wrong thing to say even while the words were jumping out of his mouth.

"I'm asking the questions. But since you brought it up, tell me why you think your friend might be in trouble."

"No reason. In this neighborhood, sometimes trouble comes knockin' on your door."

The lady cop stared at Calvin, like she could see right through him. Then she looked down at a little notebook she had open on her knee. Calvin noticed her pants were so tight there, it looked like the seams might split.

"Do you also know a Norris Palmer?"

"Huh?" Calvin tore his eyes away from the notebook and the knee. He looked at the woman's round face, trying to make himself meet her eyes. When he couldn't do it, he settled on staring at her shiny red lips. The lips moved.

"I asked you, do you know somebody by the name of Norris Palmer?"

"Yeah, I've seen him a few times."

"Know anything about him?"

"Not really."

"Isn't he Darryl Johnson's cousin?"

"Yeah. I think I might've heard somethin' 'bout that."

"Anything else you might have heard somethin' about?"

Calvin had never been questioned by a cop before. He knew he wasn't doing too good. This woman was a pro. She'd make Santa Claus feel like he had something to hide.

Albert had been standing there, listening. Now he said he needed to get back to work.

On his way out, he looked back at Calvin and said, "My advice is, just answer the questions. Don't give the officer any attitude."

The cop smiled at Albert's back as he left the room and closed the door. Calvin watched her while she adjusted her weight on the desk, leaning slightly forward and pulling on the cloth at her knees and thighs, trying to get comfortable. She looked Calvin up and down.

"Your boss is giving you good advice, Calvin."

He couldn't stand her calling him Calvin. Like they were friends.

"Look, I've worked here three years. Worked hard. Ask Albert. He even gave me a key to the place. I'm the only one of my friends with a real job that's not just a dead end."

"That's good to hear, Calvin. But it doesn't change the facts. We know there was some suspicious activity here last night. Nothing's missing. But someone reported a van parked outside, around two in the morning. We didn't get the license, but we think it belongs to Norris Palmer. You seem a little nervous, which makes me think maybe you know something."

When Calvin didn't say anything, she went on. "You and your boss both say you have a key. Is it still in your possession?"

Calvin pulled his key ring out of his pocket and showed it to her.

The cop grunted as she stood up. "Your boss says you're a good worker. Says you're smart. Too smart to get involved with something illegal."

Calvin didn't answer.

"Your boss isn't sure your friend Darryl Johnson is as smart as you."

Calvin still didn't say anything. No way he was gonna rat out Deej. He'd be happy to give her Norris P. But he couldn't figure a way to do one without the other.

The cop wrote something in her notebook, tore off the page, and handed it to Calvin.

"My name's Collins. Here's my number. You think of anything, give me a call."

"Deej is my friend," Calvin said.

The cop nodded. "Let me tell you something, Calvin. Loyalty is nice, except when it's stupid."

19

**Calvin rushed out of the shop at quitting time so he wouldn't have**
to see Albert. There was only one person he wanted to talk to. Deej.

When he got to his room, Calvin called and started talking
before Deej even said hello.

"The cops were at Albert's. Askin' questions."

"What kinda questions?"

"Like did I know you and Norris P. And did I know 'bout
somethin' suspicious happenin' last night."

"You didn't tell them nothin'. Right?"

"Right. But somebody saw the van. They called the cops,
and somehow the cops traced the van to Norris P. And somebody
called Albert this morning. Told him to check the place out. See was
anything missin'."

"Did Albert look around?"

"Yeah."

"Did he find the boxes?"

"No."

"Things'll settle down in a couple days," Deej said. "It'll be okay."

"I don't like this. You gotta find a new place, Deej."

"You want me to call Cousin Norris? Tell him you changed your
mind?"

"That's right."

"Listen to yourself, Calvin. You know that ain't gonna work."

"We gotta do somethin'."

"Look, I wanna help, but I can't. This guy in Virginia, the one
who's gonna take the boxes? That's Cousin Norris's new business
partner. No way Norris is gonna let hisself lose face in front of this
guy. If those boxes aren't right there when Norris wants 'em, he's
gonna hold me responsible. You too. You gotta understand, there's
nothin' we can do 'bout this. We gotta stay cool and let it play out."

"One week, Deej. That's what you said."

"That's right. One week."

"Okay."

"Gotta go, Calvin. I'll call you."

A week went by, and Deej didn't call. Didn't pick up his cell either. Calvin kept stopping by his house. Deej was never there. Calvin even slipped a note under the front door. Finally he went to the grocery where Granny Henry worked and asked her to have Deej call him.

Granny Henry was a tiny little woman, always glad to see Calvin when he came by the house. She seemed worried when Calvin told her he hadn't seen Deej. He could tell by the sharp way she looked at him that she had a lot of questions. But Calvin didn't have any answers. There was a line at her register, so they couldn't talk long anyway.

After nine days, Calvin went to Deej's house again. And there he was, standing in the front yard, plugged into his iPod, head moving up and down. Every few seconds he'd stop bobbing his head long enough to take a drink from a can of malt liquor he was holding. In his other hand he had a hose that was gushing water onto a beat-up looking plant.

Deej pulled off his headphones and started talking as Calvin walked up. "This here's a rosebush. Granny Henry bought it and asked me to plant it for her last fall. But she didn't say nothin' 'bout waterin' it. Think it's too late now."

"You said the boxes would be gone in a week."

"That was the plan. But Cousin Norris says now's not a good time to move 'em. They're gonna have to stay put for a while."

Deej laid the hose on the ground beside the bush, then walked over to the faucet by the porch and turned the water off. Calvin followed him, talking the whole time.

"Deej, we gotta move those boxes outta there. Albert's gonna find them. I just know it."

"There's nothin' we can do right now. We just gotta sit tight and stay cool. If you and me tried to move 'em outta there now and we got caught, that'd really be bad. Don't you see that?"

"I can't believe this is happenin'."

Deej sat down on the porch steps and stretched his legs in front of him. He took a long drink from the can and stared out at the street.

"We're just gonna have to wait till all the excitement dies down. Cousin Norris is worried 'bout it too. He's afraid if you and me get busted, you'll rat him out."

"Maybe I would."

Deej looked up. "That wouldn't be smart, Calvin."

They stared at each other. Then Deej held out the can, offering it to Calvin.

Calvin shook his head. "I don't want any."

20

**When he got home, Calvin wanted to hang out in front of the TV.**
Maybe find an action movie to take his mind off things. But Momma
was there, flipping through a magazine and watching a pet reality
show about a poodle that peed itself whenever the doorbell rang.
Little Lewis was lying on the floor, teaching himself card tricks out of
the magic kit Calvin got him for Christmas.

Calvin sprawled on the couch next to Momma. He couldn't
relax. "I can't believe you're watchin' this garbage."

Momma stopped reading and started to say something, but
Calvin was already on his feet and on his way to the kitchen. He made
himself a meatloaf sandwich and poured some chocolate milk, then
headed to his room.

As he walked through the living room, Little Lewis grabbed his
leg and said, "Hey, Calvin. Pick a card. Any card."

Calvin was definitely not in the mood for magic tricks, but he
pointed to one of the cards and said, "Okay. That one."

Little Lewis had trouble managing the cards right because his
hands were too small. Calvin watched him struggle for a while and
then ran out of patience.

"You need to practice that trick some more and show me later,"
Calvin said, his voice sounding harsher than he meant it to.

"Okay," Little Lewis said softly, letting the cards fall from his
hands.

Calvin wanted to say something else. That he was in a bad
mood. That Little Lewis shouldn't pay him no mind. But he didn't. He
just started up the stairs.

"Calvin!" Momma called after him. He didn't turn around.

He went in his room and closed the door. He put the plate on
the dresser, not hungry anymore.

Calvin lay on his bed listening to music, drinking chocolate
milk, and thinking about Junior. He hadn't seen her much lately, had
even skipped walking her to the library a few times. He told her he
was busy at work, or busy working out. He reminded her that track
season was starting in less than a month.

He missed Junior. Missed her a lot. He wanted to see her. She helped him keep his head on straight. But he didn't want her to see him when he was all knotted up inside over what he'd done.

He kept imagining those boxes sitting on the shelves in Albert's shop. Kept seeing them in his head, glowing with an evil green light, like some hidden thing in a stupid adventure movie. Like something cursed. No matter how he tried, he couldn't stop seeing them.

He really needed to spend time with Junior. And he couldn't.

What was going to happen? What if Norris P decided to leave the Blu-ray players at Albert's, knowing Albert would find them after a while and that Calvin would lose his job? What if that was Norris P's plan all along?

It was something he might do. One time Deej had told him that nothing made Cousin Norris happier than when he figured out a way to spoil things for somebody. Deej said that Norris wasn't very smart, but he always seemed to know what it was that somebody really cared about. Then he'd figure out how to take it away.

Momma walked in. Calvin pulled his headphones off.

"Do you know your little brother is lying down there on the floor, pretending he's not crying? What's got into you, boy?"

Calvin could tell she couldn't make up her mind if she was angry or worried. "I'm sorry."

"You tell him that."

"I will."

"I'll send him up." She turned to leave, but stopped in the doorway. "Is everything okay, Calvin?"

He nodded. "I got a lot on my mind. Track starts soon. Guess I'm nervous."

She came back into the room. "I'm proud of you, Calvin. For staying in school."

He forced a smile. "Yeah, looks like I'm gonna graduate."

She smiled back. It was a ninety-nine percent smile. Just a trace of worry in it. "That'll be a great day," she said.

Momma didn't say anything else for a minute, but she sat down on the bed. She put her hand on Calvin's ankle. "I hear Deej has stopped going to school."

"Yeah. A while ago."

She sat there for another few seconds, patting Calvin's foot. Finally she stood. "I'll send Little Lewis up."

About one second later, Calvin's brother was standing in the doorway, wearing a hopeful smile.

"C'mon in. I won't bite." Calvin got off the bed, searched through the mess on the floor of his closet, and found a can of old tennis balls. He popped the top off and tossed the balls to Little Lewis one at a time. He managed to catch two out of three.

"What are we gonna do?"

"I'm teachin' you to juggle. Give you somethin' to fall back on, just in case your magic career doesn't take off like you want it to."

By the time Momma called to Little Lewis that it was time for bed, he was saying, "Your juggling stinks, Calvin. I'm way better'n you!"

Calvin threw a tennis ball at his head. Little Lewis ducked and ran away laughing.

21

**Another week went by. Then Deej called Calvin late one night and** woke him up. "Cousin Norris says we can move the stuff tomorrow. Same as what we did last time."

"Just you and me?"

"Yeah. That all right with you?"

"When?"

"Two a.m. Just like before."

"Maybe we should do it a couple hours later," Calvin said. "What if somebody sees us again?"

Deej thought for a few seconds. "Nah. It'll be fine. A smooth operation. Just like the first time. Don't worry so much."

"I'll see you tomorrow night."

After he hung up, Calvin decided Deej was right. He was worrying too much. Soon the boxes would be moved, and everything would be fine.

He slept like a baby for the rest of the night and woke up feeling better than he had in a long time. He called Junior on his way to school.

"You gonna have a lotta homework tonight?" he asked.

"I don't know yet."

"I think you're gonna get a big project assigned today. You're gonna have to go back to the library after dinner and work on it."

"What if I really do have a lot of homework?"

"That's cool. I like watchin' you study. You get this cute little wrinkle between your eyebrows when you're thinkin' real hard."

Junior didn't say anything.

"I hear you smilin'," Calvin said.

"How can you hear me smiling?"

"I don't know. But you're smilin', aren't you?"

"Yes."

"I can hear it."

"What drugs are you on, boy?"

"No drugs. I'm just happy, that's all."

"I'll make up a reason to go straight home after school. So

Daddy doesn't ask why I didn't go to the library this afternoon. That way he'll have to let me go tonight."

"Sounds good."

"See you later," Junior said, the smile still in her voice. "Is seven okay?"

"I'll be there."


The rest of Calvin's day was pretty good too. He got a C on a quiz about *Othello*. Calvin hadn't read the play, but he and Junior had rented the movie and talked about it afterward.

Another thing was that Calvin ran into Coach Wilson in the hall. Coach was happy to see him and wanted to talk. "Albert says you've been practicing all winter."

"That's right."

Coach nodded. "And you're keeping up in your classes?"

"I'm doin' okay."

"Good. We've only got about twenty-five kids left on the team. Lost a bunch because of bad grades." Coach shook his head. "You know how it is, Calvin. It's the same every year."

Calvin couldn't figure out why Coach was telling him all this.

"Albert and I were talking about you yesterday. We made a decision. We picked you to be team captain. Congratulations."

Coach slapped Calvin on the back, said, "Keep up the good work," and walked on down the hall.


On his way to Albert's, Calvin was thinking about what it would be like telling Junior he was team captain. And Momma and Little Lewis. Looked like things were finally going his way for a change.

He walked into the shop and headed down the hall to the back room for some coveralls. As he passed Albert's office, Calvin noticed the door was open. He looked in because he wanted to tell Albert about his talk with Coach.

Albert was sitting at his desk, fourteen Blu-ray boxes stacked on the floor beside him.

At first, Calvin just stood there. He couldn't believe what he was seeing. There were two piles of boxes, seven in each pile. He actually counted them. Like if there were only thirteen boxes, then they weren't the same ones. They weren't his problem.

Albert looked up and saw Calvin standing in the doorway. "Explain."

"I can't," Calvin whispered, his throat suddenly dry.

"How could you do this?"

A million thoughts went through Calvin's head, but he knew there wasn't a thing he could say that would make any difference. Not to Albert, the guy who always talked about how important it was to do the right thing.

"You callin' the police?" Calvin asked.

"No."

Calvin felt his knees sag. "Why not?"

"That's a good question. I know that's what I should do." When Calvin didn't say anything, Albert went on. "Do you remember when you found that diamond earring?"

Calvin nodded. That seemed like a long time ago.

"When I called that customer and told her you found her earring, do you know what happened?"

Calvin shook his head.

"She wanted to know about you. I told her you were a good kid. She said even good kids get in trouble sometimes. And that if it ever happened to you, she wanted me to let it go the first time. She said that should be your reward for returning her earring." Albert paused. "So that's what I'm doing. I'm letting it go."

"Thank you."

"Don't thank me. I made a promise. I keep my word."

Calvin looked down. He couldn't believe this was happening.

"Everything is a test, Calvin. Remember?"

Calvin didn't say anything, just stared at the floor.

"Of course, you're fired. I can't tell you how disappointed I am."

Calvin whispered, "I'm sorry, Albert. I'm so sorry. It seemed like I had to do it. Now..."

"Now what?"

"Now, I just don't know."

"No, I guess you don't."

Albert kicked the bottom box of one of the piles, so they all jerked along the floor and moved an inch closer to Calvin.

"As for these, the last thing you are ever going to do for me is carry them outside. I don't care what happens after that. You can call Deej if you want. I assume he's mixed up in all this. He's the only person I can think of who could get you to do something this stupid."

Albert kicked the boxes another inch.

"Tell him where his stuff is. Tell him I'm not going to the police. I don't want anything more to do with this whole sorry business. I'm finished with it."

Calvin knew Albert was saying he was finished with him too.

"Three years, Calvin. How could you throw away three good years?"

"Do you want me to go now?"

Albert nodded. "Yes. But first, give me your key."

Calvin reached into his pocket and then fumbled with his key ring. It seemed like his fingers weren't working right. He held the key out to Albert.

"Put it on the desk."

Calvin put the key down.

"Evonne will mail your paycheck to you." Albert glanced at the boxes on the floor. "Don't forget to take these."

Calvin didn't move. He and Albert looked at each other for what seemed like a long time.

"What are you waiting for?"

Calvin had been hoping Albert would offer to shake his hand. Stupid.

22

**As soon as he left Albert's, Calvin called Deej. When Deej didn't**
answer, Calvin left a message saying that the Blu-rays were sitting
on the sidewalk outside Albert's, and if Deej wanted them, he better
come quick.

After he hung up, Calvin realized he didn't have anywhere to
go. He didn't have a job anymore. He couldn't go home, not this
early—Little Lewis would ask him too many questions. Junior wasn't
at the library yet. She was meeting him there in a few hours. And he
didn't have any idea where to find Deej.

Calvin decided he might as well go back to school. He had his
track stuff in his gym bag. He could change in the locker room, then
run some laps. That would make him feel better.

But when he got to school, he didn't even feel like running.
That had never happened before. He sat in the bleachers, staring at
nothing. He felt completely empty. Like there was nothing inside him
at all. Just an empty hole.

It began to rain. Calvin shivered and turned up the collar on his
jacket, but he didn't move.

Finally it started getting dark. He called Momma and told her
he wouldn't be home for dinner. Then he headed over to the library.

When Junior walked through the big wooden doors, she was
surprised Calvin was there before her. Her face lit up when she
spotted him across the big room. Then she got closer and saw his
face, his soaking wet jacket.

She sat down beside him, touched his arm, and whispered,
"What happened?"

He started to tell her, but the librarian hurried over and told
them they had to leave if they were going to talk. Calvin picked up
Junior's backpack, and they pushed their way through the doors to the
outside.

The rain had settled into a steady March downpour. But the
building was old and had a wide porch that kept them dry. They stood
near one of the dirty white columns while Calvin told his story.

When she'd heard everything, Junior put her arms around

Calvin's neck and pulled his head down so their foreheads touched.

"Oh, baby. I'm so sorry," she said.

It helped Calvin just to be near her. He felt better, but he knew it wouldn't last.

"At least Albert didn't call the police," Junior said. "That would be terrible."

Calvin didn't answer.

"Maybe he'll give you another chance."

"Why should he?"

"But he said he knew it was Deej that got you into this. Daddy always said Deej was a bad influence."

Calvin pulled away from her. "I don't wanna talk about Deej."

"Calvin, I love you. I don't want anything bad to happen."

"I love you too."

"You need to stop being friends with Deej."

"Junior, I just lost my job. Albert wouldn't even shake my hand when he told me to leave. And now you're givin' me a hard time. I don't need this right now."

"Maybe what happened is a good thing. After all the trouble Deej has made for you, now you can see. He's not good enough for you."

"Deej will always be my friend."

"Calvin, he's dragging you down. Why can't you see that?" Junior was crying now. She reached out for Calvin, but he didn't move.

"This is your daddy talkin', isn't it?"

"No. He doesn't even know about this."

"I bet he said it before. When I got suspended. Didn't he?"

"He said he thought Deej was headed for trouble and he hoped you didn't get involved. But you did. So Daddy was right."

Calvin grabbed the handle on the library's heavy door and yanked it open. "You know what, Junior? You should go back to your books and your nice school and your daddy. Go back to where everything is easy and safe. That's where girls like you belong. Go on! Get out of here!"

He stood holding the door, glaring at her. Finally Junior picked up her backpack and ran inside.

Afterward, Calvin paced around the columns on the porch, muttering to himself like a crazy street person. Then he went inside to find her.

He saw Junior hurrying into the women's restroom. He went back to the porch to wait. She'd have to come out sooner or later.

He'd talk to her. Apologize. Tell her he didn't know what he was doing. Didn't know what he was saying. That he was all mixed up. That she was the only good thing left in his life.

Fifteen minutes later, Junior walked out the door. Right away, Calvin was at her side. "I'm sorry, Junior. I didn't mean it. Don't go. Please!"

But she didn't stop. She was crying and running down the sidewalk, and here was her father's SUV pulling up to the curb. Calvin watched as she got in and the car drove away, red taillights shining through the rain.

He stepped back into the shadows of the porch and leaned against one of the columns. Hidden in the darkness, Calvin slid down until he was huddled on the ground, his arms covering his head.

The next day Junior left a message on his phone. She was crying. "I'm so sorry, Calvin. Daddy says I can't see you anymore."

23

**The next two weeks were as bad as when Daddy Lewis died. Maybe** worse, since Calvin knew he'd brought it all on himself.

He kept calling Junior. She never answered. He left long messages. She didn't call back. Calvin was afraid to go to her house.

But he had to see her. So one afternoon he waited across the street from Saint Bernadette's until the final bell rang and the students started pouring out the front doors. Even mixed in with hundreds of girls all dressed the same, Junior was easy to spot.

She came down the steps, walking slowly. She was alone, not surrounded by a bunch of her friends. Calvin hoped she would at least talk to him.

He had already started across the street when he saw her father's car pull up to the curb. Junior climbed in. Calvin finally understood what was happening. Junior's daddy was making sure Calvin never spoke to his daughter again.

That night, while Calvin was lifting weights, Little Lewis came downstairs to watch. He brought a deck of cards so he could practice his tricks.

Calvin kind of liked having him there. For one thing, Little Lewis was always impressed with how strong Calvin was. Plus having him around helped distract Calvin from thinking about the mess he'd made of everything.

Little Lewis settled himself into an old beanbag chair. At first he just played with his cards, every once in a while looking over at Calvin doing bench presses.

Then he asked, "How come you don't still see Junior?"

Calvin didn't answer, just grunted like he was working extra hard to finish his reps.

Little Lewis said it again. "How come you don't still see Junior?'"

"We broke up." Calvin said it while he toweled off so Little Lewis couldn't see his face.

"Why?"

"Junior was givin' me a hard time. Said Deej was no good."

"She doesn't know what she's talkin' 'bout."

"That's what I told her."

"You and Deej have been friends since before I was born."

"That's right."

Little Lewis started poking his finger into a hole in the chair's yellow plastic cover.

"You make that hole bigger and the beans all come out, Momma's gonna be real mad at you."

Little Lewis stuck his hands into his armpits. "Deej is the man. He treats me like I'm his little brother."

"I know."

"Sometimes he's nicer to me than you are, Calvin."

"That's right. He is."

Little Lewis went back to shuffling his cards around while Calvin started another set. "So how come Deej isn't around like he used to be?"

Instead of answering, Calvin made a production of adding another weight to the bar.

"Did you and Deej have a fight too?"

"No. He's just busy, that's all."

"Junior shouldn't have said that about Deej."

Calvin kept lifting and didn't answer.

"Deej is your best friend."

No answer.

Little Lewis said, "There's other girls."

"Not for me."

There was silence then, except for the sound of Calvin grunting as he struggled to finish the set. Then his cell phone rang.

"I'm not done here," Calvin managed to say to his brother. "Check caller ID and see who it is."

Little Lewis picked up Calvin's phone and read the screen. "Mal-vin-a Henry. Who's that?"

"That's Deej's granny." Calvin dropped the bar into the rack with a clang and grabbed the phone. "Hey, Granny Henry. Everything okay?"

There was a pause at the other end, then a quiet voice saying, "Oh, Calvin. It finally happened. Deej is in jail."

24

**Calvin's first priority was taking care of Granny Henry, Deej's**
Number One Girl. He knew that's what Deej would want him to do.
So when she asked Calvin to come to the arraignment with her in a few
days, he said yes.

Granny Henry said she wasn't sure what the day would be like,
but she needed somebody steady who'd do whatever might need doing.
Not give her an argument like Shania or get hysterical like Danette.

The arraignment was on a Tuesday. That meant Calvin would
have to skip school. At first he thought he would just skip without
saying anything to Momma. But he had been screwing things up so
much lately, he decided to tell her. Not ask her, tell her. He wanted her
to understand that this was something he was going to do whether she
said it was okay or not.

When he told Momma about it, she surprised him and said,
"You should go. It's the right thing to do."

Calvin was glad to hear he was doing the right thing for a change.

The day of the arraignment, Shania drove her Camry up to Calvin's
house, and he climbed in back beside Danette. Then he leaned across
the front seat and squeezed Granny Henry's skinny shoulder through
her green wool coat. She patted his hand.

"Thank you for coming, Calvin."

"How was Deej when he called?"

"He sounded scared."

Danette burst into loud sobs.

"Stop it, Danette, or I swear I'm gonna make you get out the
car and walk," Shania threatened. "You just makin' things worse."

"Did he say what happened?" Calvin asked, ignoring Danette.

Granny Henry sat quietly and stared out the window, her hands
folded in her lap. At first Calvin thought she wasn't going to answer.

"I can't remember everything. He said he was driving a stolen
car. The police stopped him. But he drove off. So they chased him
until they caught him again." Her voice trailed away, and she went
back to looking out of the window.

Calvin let her be. He sat back in his seat, and they rode in silence the rest of the way, except for the sound of Danette sniffling and blowing her nose.

At the courthouse, Deej's court-appointed lawyer sat with them on a hard wooden bench in the hall outside the hearing room. The lawyer was young, wore heavy black glasses and a suit with too-short sleeves. He didn't have any style, but he was respectful to Granny Henry, and Calvin liked that.

Right away, Granny Henry asked the lawyer, "Where's Deej? Can I see him?"

"Not until they bring him out, Mrs. Henry."

Granny Henry pressed her lips together and nodded once.

The lawyer said, "Now, I want to be sure you understand what's going to happen. First the Assistant U.S. Attorney will read the charges. Then the judge will ask some questions. And then he'll decide if Darryl will be detained or released until the trial."

"So he might come home?"

"Probably not, Mrs. Henry. For one thing, Darryl's nineteen. In the eyes of the law, he's an adult. Plus he already tried to run when he drove away from the police the first time they stopped him. So they probably won't let him out on bail."

Danette started crying.

The lawyer continued, "I want you to realize, the charges against your grandson are very serious. According to the report, when he was trying to escape from the police in the stolen car, he crashed into two other vehicles."

Granny Henry's lips tightened and she turned her head away.

"Is that everything?" Calvin asked.

"No, unfortunately. After Darryl crashed the car, he tried to back up and drive away. A police officer had gotten out of his patrol car and was standing behind the car Darryl was driving."

"He ran over a cop?" Shania asked.

"No, he didn't hit the officer. But there is some question about whether he tried. Naturally we believe he did not see the policeman in his rearview mirror. We'll try to get the judge to understand the state of mind your grandson was in at the time. That he just panicked and backed up without looking. Are you following all this, Mrs. Henry?"

"Yes, I am." She paused. "What's going to happen to my boy?"

"I don't know yet, ma'am. I was pleased to find out that he has no police record. He hasn't even been arrested before. That should be a point in his favor."

Granny Henry sat up straighter and got a little pride in her voice. "My Deej has always been a good boy."

The lawyer nodded. "I'm sure that's true, Mrs. Henry. But in this case, there's no question that he did most of the things he's been charged with. My advice to him will be to plead guilty to most of the charges. That will avoid a trial, and it usually means a lesser sentence. I will try to get the judge to drop the charge involving driving his car at a police officer."

By now Danette was crying loudly. Granny Henry opened her purse and gave a tissue to Calvin. "Pass that to Danette. And tell her to hush."

The arraignment didn't last long. Deej came in. He wore an orange prison jumpsuit that was too big for him.

He walked slowly, with his head down. He kept looking over at the corrections officer beside him, waiting to be told where to go.

The corrections officer walked Deej over to the table where his lawyer sat. While Deej was sitting down, he looked around the courtroom and saw Calvin and Granny Henry, along with his sisters.

When he looked at Calvin, Deej's face didn't change. But when he looked at Granny Henry, he gave her a little smile that looked like it hurt him to make it. Then he turned away and didn't look at them again.

Deej and his lawyer put their heads together and talked quietly for a few minutes. After that the judge came in and everybody stood up.

The judge got right to business. He looked through the papers in front of him. Then he looked up at Deej, called him by his full name, Darryl Johnson, and told him to stand up while the charges were read.

Unauthorized use of a vehicle. Resisting arrest. Operating a vehicle in an unsafe manner. Attempting to leave the scene of an accident. Possible vehicular assault of a police officer.

Calvin stared at Deej's back while the words were read. He watched Deej's head sink lower with each new charge. The legal words were long and complicated, but you didn't have to understand all of it to know Deej was in a whole lot of trouble.

25

**A few days later, Granny Henry called Calvin to say she didn't need** him to come with her to court for Deej's sentencing. She was all right, now that the shock had worn off.

Afterward she called back and told Calvin that the judge had given Deej eighteen months. This was what the lawyer had told them to expect, but still Calvin couldn't believe it.

Whenever he thought of Deej being locked up, Calvin had trouble breathing. It was how he felt sometimes after a hard session running up and down the bleachers, when he was gasping for air but his lungs wouldn't fill up. Like they weren't working right.

And Calvin started to think about what it would be like if he was in jail. He knew the worst thing would be not being able to run. Not ever being allowed to just take off at top speed, seeing how long he could keep it up before he had to slow down. What would it be like knowing he couldn't run for a year and a half? What was it like for Deej?

The day after Granny Henry called, track season started. It was finally here. The season Calvin had dreamed about for so long. Calvin was team captain. And Deej was in jail.

It was the first practice, so the coaches didn't bother with their stopwatches. They just watched the kids. Everybody ran. The hurdlers went over the low hurdles, working a little on their timing. Coach Wilson had Calvin and the other sprinters run a few practice sprints, but not full out. Calvin was holding back a lot, but Coach got excited anyway when he saw how fast he was. Calvin kept looking over at Albert, wanting a smile or a nod. Something.

When practice ended, Calvin stayed to help Albert put the equipment away, just like always. Usually, while they carried the hurdles and stacked them together along the side of the track, Albert would be talking to Calvin, giving his views on things. But this time he didn't say anything.

Finally words just flew out of Calvin's mouth. "Looks like Deej will be spending some time in jail."

Albert arranged the last hurdle the way he wanted it and then looked at Calvin. "I'm sorry to hear that."

"You said it was gonna happen. I didn't believe you."

"That's because he's your friend."

Calvin wanted to keep Albert talking. "How are things at the shop? César doin' okay?"

"He's fine."

"How's Zipper?"

"I thought you might have heard. Zipper's dead."

"What?"

"Somebody fed him a sandwich with rat poison in it."

"Rat poison!"

"Happened two weeks ago."

"Why would somebody wanna do that?"

"I think maybe they never got their Blu-ray players back," Albert said. "Probably someone else took them. Deej's friends must've been mad about that. So they poisoned Zipper. It was pure meanness."

"But Deej is in jail, so it wasn't his fault."

"Not directly."

Calvin didn't say anything, just stood there shaking his head, imagining Albert coming in one morning and finding Zipper dead.

"Zipper was a really great dog, Albert. I'm sorry." He paused, then added, "About everything."

"I'm sorry too, Calvin."

It felt good to be talking to Albert again. Calvin had more to say, but he couldn't find the words.

"I wish I could make it stop," he finally said.

"Make what stop?"

"I did a stupid thing. 'Cause I wanted to help Deej. And my head was all messed up. So I didn't think things through, didn't realize all the bad stuff that might happen."

Albert didn't say anything, but Calvin could tell he was listening.

"You fired me. And Deej went to jail. I thought nothing else could happen. But I was wrong. Junior broke up with me." Calvin paid no attention to Albert's look of surprise, just kept talking. "And now this thing with Zipper. The bad things haven't stopped."

"What's done is done, Calvin. You messed up. But you didn't mess up like Deej did. You're not in jail. You're going to graduate. You might even win the championship. You looked good out there today. Stay focused on that."

"I looked good?" Calvin asked.

But Albert was already walking away.

26

**Calvin lit up the track that spring. He won every race. Some meets,** he'd knock a hundredth of a second off his time to get a new PB. Personal Best. There was even some talk about him in the local news.

Nobody but Calvin knew what was making him run so fast. It wasn't just that he had trained hard all year. That he was mentally ready for each race. That he always pushed himself to run his hardest. That it was his last season. The real reason was Deej.

Calvin hadn't been able to see Deej yet because there was some mix-up and Granny Henry still hadn't got him on Deej's visitors list. But Deej had managed to call him one time.

"Hey, Calvin. It's me."

"Hey, man! I can't believe it's really you."

"Well, it is."

Calvin decided Deej sounded just the same as before. Maybe quieter. But then Calvin wondered if Deej might have been working hard to sound like he hadn't changed. Calvin couldn't tell without seeing his face.

"How you doin'?" Calvin asked.

"It's okay. There's rules. You know? I don't mean prison rules. I'm talkin' 'bout the inmate rules. The rules they have for each other. Long as you don't break those, you're okay."

That was as much as Deej would say about being in jail. After that, all he wanted to talk about was Calvin and what the news was saying about him. He asked Calvin to describe each race he'd run, who the other sprinters were, how Calvin had felt during the race, what his time was. It seemed like Calvin winning the 100-meter dash in the championship meant everything to Deej.

The D.C. Track Championship would last two days. All the qualifying events happened on Tuesday. The finals were Wednesday.

Momma and Calvin agreed that she and Little Lewis wouldn't come the first day. The day that mattered was Wednesday. That's when Calvin wanted them there, to watch him win the biggest race of his life.

He wanted Junior there too. Ever since they started going out, he'd always thought she would be there. He'd daydreamed about her sitting in the stands next to Momma and Little Lewis, looking fine, cheering him on, hugging and kissing him after he won. It hurt, knowing that Junior would never see him race. But there was no point even thinking about that now.

The night before the qualifying events, Momma cooked a big pasta dinner. Calvin wasn't that hungry, but he made himself eat. He knew he'd need the energy later, and he didn't want to hurt Momma's feelings.

As soon as dinner was over, Calvin went up to his room to lie down with his headphones on and stare at the ceiling fan over his bed. He must have fallen asleep for a few hours. When he woke up, the house was dark and quiet. The clock said one in the morning.

Calvin got out of bed and repacked his gym bag one last time. Made sure he had everything. Track shoes, tracksuit, extra socks, energy bars, power drinks, his warm-up jacket with Team Captain written across the back.

He wished he could call Deej. Deej always knew how to calm him down the night before a big race. He wondered if Deej was awake too, thinking about Calvin. He figured he probably was, and that helped him relax. It wasn't as good as Deej really being there, but it was something anyway.

Since he was too wound up to sleep, Calvin decided to go over to the track. He knew if he ran a few laps, nice and slow, it would help him calm down.

Calvin started smiling to himself as soon as he set foot on the track. At first he just walked, hands in the pockets of his hoodie. Then he started jogging. He felt good.

Even in the dark, he knew every straightaway, every curve. Just like he knew the shape of his own foot. It was a kind of recognition that happened deep inside.

He kept himself to an easy trot. He didn't bother counting how many times he went around. Three or four. That was all. Then he stopped. He was still smiling. He was ready.

As he headed out the gate, he saw a dark shape in the

bleachers. Someone was sitting near the aisle, about ten rows up. Then the shape moved, and Calvin saw a flicker of light reflecting off a shaved head bent low toward a cigarette. Calvin's heart froze. He knew who it was, even before the soft voice reached his ears.

"Hey, Runner Boy."

Calvin didn't move, didn't speak. Left it to Norris to climb off the bleachers and come toward him.

When Norris reached Calvin, he stood close and said, "Glad you finally showed. Otherwise we was gonna have to have this talk tomorrow before the meet." He took a slow drag from his cigarette. "Been to see Deej?"

"Not yet."

"I saw him. We had a few things to talk over. Remember that deal you and me made, back in August?"

Calvin nodded.

"Remind me what the deal was, Calvin."

"The deal was that you own my knees."

"That's right. But now we got a different deal."

"A different deal?"

"Yeah. That's what I said. What's the matter, boy, you slow or somethin'?"

"Tell me the deal."

"Your part of the deal is the same. You're still gonna lose the championship. So don't get your hopes up none 'bout that. But the consequences..." Norris drew the word out, making it last a long time. "I like that word, don't you, Calvin?" Norris smiled and said it again. "The *consequences* is that if you don't lose, somethin' bad is gonna happen to Deej."

"What're you talkin' 'bout? Somethin' bad already happened to Deej. Or didn't you know that? He's in jail. 'Cause of what he was doin' for you."

"Deej is in jail 'cause he panicked and got caught."

"You can't get to him."

"What makes you think I can't hurt Deej just 'cause he's in jail?" Norris leaned forward and poked his finger into Calvin's chest. "Here's what your knees are gonna do. They're gonna win the qualifying race tomorrow so's you get in the finals. Then you know what happens? Your knees are gonna lose. You got that, Runner Boy? You're gonna lose the big race. The championship."

Calvin didn't say anything, just willed Norris to go away. Leave him alone. But Norris wasn't finished.

"You do that, nothin' bad is gonna happen to Deej." He paused. "You don't do what I say? Who knows what might go down."

"But he's your cousin."

"The whole family already won't have nothin' to do with me 'cause of what happened to Deej. Turns out he was everybody's favorite."

Norris leaned closer to Calvin. He was worked up now, spraying spit into Calvin's face.

"Know what else? I'm not even bettin' on that race. Decided not to. I just wanna see you lose. You got that?"

Norris got himself under control, took his finger out of Calvin's chest. Grinning now, he bent over and talked to Calvin's legs.

"Hey, knees! You hear what I'm sayin'? You gonna lose the last race of your running career. The big one. Are you listenin' to me, knees?"

He straightened up, the smile gone.

"I mean it, Runner Boy. You better lose."

27

**Harry Truman High School never had enough money for a bus to** take the team to the championship, but this year was different. This year, the team had a lot of good runners. The new starting blocks had made everybody faster. Calvin was almost certain to win. The team was expected to place in the top three schools. And somehow Coach Wilson and Albert managed to borrow two big vans so they could drive the whole team to the meet.

The kids were excited. This way they'd be rested and relaxed when they got there, instead of stressed out from getting up early and riding an hour on the Metro.

Because he was team captain, Calvin was first to get on the van. He took a spot in the back corner, put his headphones on, and pretended to sleep, using his gym bag for a pillow.

He didn't want to think about anything, especially his conversation with Norris P.

Calvin used the music to push the problem from his mind. He figured it was okay for now. Today, even Norris P wanted him to run fast and get into the finals. But Calvin still didn't know what he was going to do about tomorrow. When he thought about it, he felt sick. Like he could throw up.

Later. He'd worry about it later.

Calvin kept his eyes closed the whole ride. But he was aware of the van moving slowly through morning traffic.

About an hour later, he felt the van turn off the street and drive across a field. It bumped along the uneven ground for a while and then stopped. He sensed people moving around him and opened his eyes.

Ashlee, one of the girls on the team, was leaning over him and smiling. "Hey, Calvin. We're here. You okay?"

He faked a stretch and gave her a smile. "Just stayin' relaxed, Ash."

Calvin climbed down from the van. The second his feet touched the ground, he got a jolt of adrenaline. Just like always. It was as if there was an electric current running through the ground, and Calvin's feet started buzzing as soon as there was contact.

The team worked quickly to put up the nylon shelter Albert had brought along, a place to sit out of the sun between races. Except for when they went close to cheer each other on, they'd spend most of the day resting under the tent, waiting for their events to come up.

There was always a lot of waiting at a track meet. Hours of sitting around for a few minutes to prove you were the best. Running. Jumping. Throwing. You just wanted your chance.

Once the tent was up, Coach Wilson and Albert gathered the team together. Coach wasn't a big talker, so his speech was short.

"Welcome to the D.C. Championship! Now, I don't want anybody getting nervous."

Some of the kids laughed.

"I mean it. It'll slow you down. You feel yourself tensing up, go see Calvin. This is his fourth championship. He's a pro at staying loose. He'll help you out.

"I posted the schedule of events in the tent. There's a big clock there too. Pay attention to the time. Those of you with early events, start warming up now. If you're not in the first heats, you can relax for a while." He looked at Albert. "Do you have anything to add?"

Albert smiled. "Not really. Remember to warm up about an hour before your event. The rest of the time, you should stay hydrated and in the shade. Too much sun will sap your energy and slow you down. Stay focused. Try your best. And remember to enjoy yourselves."

After that, most of the team went off to the tent to find a spot and settle in. The girls started their ritual of braiding each other's hair. Sometimes one of the guys would ask for a comb-out and a rebraid. The girls were happy to do it. They liked fussing over the boys, over each other.

There was a lot of physical contact in the tent. When the guys and girls walked around, they'd bump into each other on purpose. They sat with their arms hanging around each other's necks. It made them feel good, being totally comfortable with each other. Getting juiced up from being together, from being part of the team.

And I'm team captain, Calvin thought. They all look to me. I'm supposed to be the one with all the answers. If they only knew.

The day went by in a blur. Calvin tried to keep himself busy. He helped the other runners warm up, stretch, keep calm, stay focused.

Then he had to do the same thing for himself.

He won his preliminary heat in 11.04. He won his semi in 11.03. Fast. And faster. Just like he planned it.

In the van on the way home, Calvin leaned against the window, his team jacket over his head, so nobody would even think about bothering him. They all thought he was asleep.

He felt like a character in a movie. He tried to think about different ways the movie might turn out. But he'd never been any good at figuring out the future. That's why his life was such a mess. Why being fast was the only thing he had left. All he wanted was to stay in the dark world behind his jacket and never come out.

28

**The vans dropped everybody at school, and Calvin walked home.**
Little Lewis was waiting for him out on the sidewalk. He grabbed
Calvin's gym bag and carried it up the steps.

"How was it?" Little Lewis asked.

"I'm in the finals."

Momma was smiling on the porch. "How fast was your time?"
she asked.

"Fast enough."

Calvin walked past her and into the house. He started climbing
the stairs to his room.

Momma and Little Lewis followed him inside.

"You okay, Calvin?" Momma called out.

"Fine."

"You want anything?"

"Not right now."

"Let me know if you do."

Calvin didn't answer. But he did glance over his shoulder at
Momma standing with her hand on the stair rail, her face turned up,
and Little Lewis beside her, looking worried.

Calvin lay down on his bed and stared up at the fan spinning in
slow circles above him. Usually the fan relaxed him. But this time, it
made him feel like his brain was spinning too. He closed his eyes, but
his brain kept going.

The room grew dark. At some point Little Lewis tiptoed in. Calvin
opened his eyes and saw his brother standing right there next to him,
holding a plate with both hands, trying hard to be careful with it.

"Momma thought maybe you might be hungry," Little Lewis
whispered.

"Looks good, little brother." Calvin glanced at the plate of
sandwiches and fruit and managed a smile. "Put it on the dresser. I'll
get to it later."

Little Lewis hunched his shoulders up around his ears and let
the words tumble out in a rush. "Momma says to tell you we know
you can do it. We believe in you."

When Calvin didn't say anything, Little Lewis stood there another few seconds, eyes big. Then he ran out of the room. Calvin groaned and rolled over.

A minute later, his cell phone rang.

"Hey, Calvin."

"Deej! It's after nine o'clock. How'd you get 'em to let you call so late?"

"There's this guard. I told him about you. He's lettin' me use his phone. But we just got a couple minutes. How you holdin' up? Feelin' relaxed? Tomorrow's the big day."

Calvin sat up, rolled his shoulders. "I'm a little tense. Wish you was here to help take my mind off things."

"Wish I was too, brother. Always thought I would be."

There was silence.

"Listen, Deej. I got this problem."

"I know."

"You know?" Calvin said.

"Yeah. Norris talked to me. Came to see me yesterday."

"I don't know what to do, Deej."

"Yes, you do."

"No. I don't. I really don't."

"You gotta win, Calvin."

"You're crazy! Norris P is gonna send somebody after you."

"I been gettin' a whole lotta visitors. Did I tell you Granny Henry came to see me today?"

"Deej, we gotta talk about this."

Deej ignored him. "She was so old and sad, I didn't hardly wanna look at her. She just kept pattin' my hand and sayin', 'You're a good boy, Deej.' "

Calvin didn't say anything.

"After she left, I started thinkin'. I asked myself—Am I good? Am I bad? I don't know. I never set out to be bad. One thing I do know, me bein' your friend ain't brought you nothin' but trouble."

"Don't say that."

"Except for a couple times, you stood by me more'n I stood by you."

"That's not true."

"Don't throw the race 'cause of me, Calvin."

"They're gonna hurt you, Deej."

"I been thinkin' 'bout this, Calvin. You gotta win. Win for both of us. Show Norris he can't just step on people's dreams. Runnin' is what you do better'n anybody else."

"But Deej..."

"Don't worry 'bout me. I can take care of myself. You win that race. You got that?"

"Deej!"

Deej was gone, but Calvin sat there, the phone still pressed against his ear.

29

**The next morning, as soon as Calvin got to the meet, he went**
looking for Albert. "Can I talk to you for a minute?"

Something in Calvin's voice made Albert look up from his
clipboard and give Calvin his full attention.

"I think it would be better if I didn't win today."

"Calvin! What do you mean?"

"I can't explain. There's this situation."

"When are you going to stop getting caught in these
'situations'?"

"I think this is the last time. I really do."

"Can you tell me what's going on?"

"Somethin' bad is gonna happen if I win."

"Is your friend Deej part of this?"

"It's not his fault this time."

"You're saying you'd walk away from your chance to win? Can you
do that? Are you sure you even want to? Because you need to be sure."

"I keep messin' up, Albert. And I think it's 'cause I don't try
hard enough to figure things out ahead of time."

"So that's what you're trying to do? Figure things out?"

"That's right. I've thought about it. I decided I can live without
winning the championship. If it means protecting a friend. Somebody
who'd do the same for me."

"Sounds like you've made up your mind."

"I know I'd be lettin' down a lotta people. Trouble is, track is
just about the only thing I haven't messed up. I wanted to get it right
for once."

"Calvin, don't forget how hard you worked for this. The whole
team is counting on you."

Calvin's head hung lower. He should have known. Albert never
made things easy.

"Calvin, what if I said to you, 'Life is understood backward'?
Would you know what I was talking about?"

Calvin took his time before he answered. "I guess it's sayin'
sometimes you don't understand something till it's over?"

"That's it," Albert said. "That's exactly it."

Albert looked around at all the activity, at the officials rushing around the field and the athletes warming up, but Calvin knew he wasn't seeing them.

"You know, Calvin, sometimes when I have a hard decision to make, I try to pretend I'm an old man, and I'm looking back at the things I did and I'm asking myself, 'Is that something I'd do again? What did I end up losing on account of that choice? Who did I hurt?' Does that help, Calvin?"

"Maybe. I'm not really sure. But thanks, Albert."

Albert offered his hand. They shook. "Anytime, Calvin."

30

**Calvin's event wasn't until the afternoon, so he spent his time** getting his teammates ready. Helping them stretch. Talking to them. Making little jokes. Keeping them loose.

Then it was time to get ready himself. As he retied his track shoes one last time, he looked up into the stands. The bleachers had been filling slowly since lunchtime, for the big races at the end of the day.

Calvin could pick out Momma in her bright orange dress and her floppy sunhat. And there was Little Lewis beside her, waving whenever he thought Calvin was looking.

He saw Norris too. He was sitting by himself up in the last row, leaning forward with his elbows on his knees, heavy chains on his wrists, hands dangling. His designer shades were turned on Calvin.

Calvin made himself look away and concentrate on his warm-up. He always followed the same routine. Touched his toes. Jogged in place. Did jumpies, side stretches, some high kicks. Stretched out his quads and hamstrings. Tried out his start position to make sure his shoes felt right.

Some of his teammates came up to wish him luck. He didn't pay much attention. They didn't expect him to. They all knew what it was like before a race. There was a place in your head that helped you run your fastest. You needed to find that place.

Coach Wilson came up. "I saw you talking with Albert. I don't have much to add. Just that you've been a great captain. The other kids really look up to you. I know you'll make us proud."

The announcer called the next event. The men's 100-meter dash. Calvin walked out onto the track, took his spot in lane four. The other runners lined up on either side.

He knew what he had to do. He felt calm.

Everything slowed down. Calvin leaned over and placed his hands on the ground, then put his feet in the starting blocks.

He took a deep breath in, then slowly let it out, his lips silently forming the words, "This one's for you, Deej."

The gun went off, and the runners surged forward.

Calvin had a good start. He kept his head down for the drive, his legs pounding the track like two pistons. His arms were punching forward, grabbing the air and helping pull him toward the finish line.

He was flying.

## Acknowledgments

Special thanks to Heleny Cook at Wilson High School, who opened her classroom to me, and to Coach Green for letting me hang out with the track team. Wilson impressed me as a place with many hardworking students and teachers. The worn-out school depicted in my book is not a place I ever visited.

Thanks to all the people who read and commented on the work as it began to take shape. To Judy Morris, who was my first reader and encouraged me to keep going. To the members of my fantastic writer's group, Sharon, Karen, Miriam, Sandy, Annika, Virginia, and Mary: you never failed to give me good advice. To Ellen Olmstead and Charlie Temple, who provided careful feedback and assured me I was on track. And to Elijah, who paid me the highest compliment of all when he said, "I felt like you were writing about me."

Heartfelt gratitude to my editor and publisher, Stephen Roxburgh.

Many years of thanks to my husband, John, and our children, Elizabeth and Wilson, whose unflagging support and interest meant so much to me. They never stopped believing I could do it, but must have wondered why it was taking so long.

Thank you.